A warning bell clamored in her mind

What am I doing, Evy wondered. She pushed herself up slightly and tried to separate herself mentally from the strange sensations Jason was arousing in her. Nothing seemed to work.

"Stop trying to analyze it. Let yourself go," Jason said.

"I can't do that," she said glumly. Nothing in her life had ever been successfully accomplished by letting herself go. "I really thought I'd become a practiced hero in these past four weeks, but it's not true. I've had too many years of cowardly living behind me to make such a sudden change. I'm sorry, Jason, but there it is."

"It's just too soon," Jason murmured in her ear. "I can see the devil in you, Evy Hart. All I have to do is figure how to get it out."

Books by Emma Goldrick

HARLEQUIN PRESENTS
688—AND BLOW YOUR HOUSE DOWN
791—MISS MARY'S HUSBAND
825—NIGHT BELLS BLOOMING

HARLEQUIN ROMANCE
2661—THE ROAD

These books may be available at your local bookseller.

Don't miss any of our special offers. Write to us at the following address for information on our newest releases.

Harlequin Reader Service
P.O. Box 52040, Phoenix, AZ   85072-2040
Canadian address: P.O. Box 2800, Postal Station A,
5170 Yonge St., Willowdale, Ont.   M2N 6J3

EMMA GOLDRICK

night bells blooming

Harlequin Books

TORONTO • NEW YORK • LONDON
AMSTERDAM • PARIS • SYDNEY • HAMBURG
STOCKHOLM • ATHENS • TOKYO • MILAN

Harlequin Presents first edition October 1985
ISBN 0-373-10825-7

Original hardcover edition published in 1985
by Mills & Boon Limited

CHAPTER ONE

I⠀T was there the moment she turned around, and waves of fear roiled her stomach as they had not done since Frank had—but this was different. The world seemed to stand still on the sunny plaza of Santiago de Puerto Rico, in the middle of the Sunday siesta. Not a whisper of a breeze ruffled the stately royal palms that guarded the church of San Fernando. Even the fountain in the middle of the plaza seemed frozen. The heavy scent of jasmine, and the cloying odour of the frangipani, oranges, and coffee extract weighed down the tropical air.

She had seen the movement out of the corner of her eye. An elderly mongrel dog, chasing its tail in the seventy-eight-degree weather. Nothing else lived on the plaza except for herself and the dog. And when she made a full turn to look closely, she knew there was reason to be fearful. The dog had stopped its circling, and now stood stiffly, glaring at her. All around its grey muzzle there was a collar of white foam.

The animal took two tottering steps in her direction. It was enough to throw her mind completely out of control. She dropped her briefcase on the sidewalk in front of the wooden bench that comprised the bus stop, and raised both hands to her mouth to cut off the whimpering moan that was rising beyond her control.

The dog's head swayed, as if the animal stood in a great wind. Evy took two short steps backward, eyes fixed on the slavering mouth. And then she screamed, wild and untended, shaking the siesta attitude of the little city, causing the flock of somnolent pigeons to go winging off into the forested mountain above the town. A head appeared around the massive front door of the church across the square. Two more looked out from the cantina down the street. But Evy was oblivious to it all. She saw only the rabid dog. She took two more backward steps into the street, squarely into the path of the Continental that had swung around the corner behind her, unseen.

The brakes on the big car squealed, and the back end tailfished as the driver swung the front wheels outward, away from her. The hood of the car barely missed her, but the bumper caught at her skirt, twirling her around. Off balance, she fell awkwardly backward on to the hood of the halted car, and promptly fainted.

Barely minutes later she returned to consciousness, to find herself sprawled half in and half out of the front seat of the car. Her broad-brimmed sun hat had been lost in the confusion, and her mass of long blonde hair had cascaded down her back. Her demure skirt was hiked up high on her lightly-tanned thigh, and a man was leaning over her. She shuddered, and scrambled away from him. The dog was forgotten; the man himself had become the centre of her fear. It was the way of fear, the psychiatrist had told her. First you fear the one thing that has frightened you, then you learn to fear everything surrounding that thing, and, if you don't fight back, you come to fear everything. Fight back, her brain told her. Fight back against the fear!

'What—what?' she stammered.

'I don't know,' he returned harshly. 'It looked as if you were trying to commit suicide by walking backwards into my car.' It was a deep voice, laden with sarcasm, as if he wanted to add, 'And what would you expect from a dizzy blonde?'

'The dog?' she asked weakly.

'Don't worry about the dog. How about you?'

'I—I'm all right,' she said. Her hip felt bruised, as did her left leg, but no major nerves were complaining. She struggled to sit up and to pull down her skirt at the same time. 'The dog?' she repeated. The man's head almost blotted out her view, but she could tell that behind him twenty or thirty people had appeared almost by magic, and were crowding around the car.

'What dog?' the man asked. Evy shook her head, trying to clear her mind, but only succeeded in scattering her loose silky hair around her head and into his face. As she fumbled to regain control of herself she assessed him. A broad well-tanned face, clean-shaven, with dark eyes and black curly hair. Heavy eyebrows that seemed to move when he spoke, and in the middle of the left eyebrow, a tuft of white hair, sticking straight up. Fine teeth. Tall enough to lean over her at head level, even though his feet were in the gutter. He was dressed casually. Light grey slacks, and an open-collar white shirt—typical for the February sunshine of the island. She gulped, and purposefully spoke loudly enough to be heard on the fringes of the crowd.

'There was a dog,' she said, her voice quivering and shaking. 'A mongrel dog. He came towards me with his mouth foaming—rabies, I think.' Instantly the word was picked up and repeated. '*Rabia!*' she could hear someone yell. '*Un perro loco!*' Just as swiftly as the crowd had gathered, it disappeared. Behind them, a street away, a gun cracked twice, and was silent.

'Well, you certainly know how to break up a crowd!' the man laughed. 'Now, let's check you out.' He swung both of her feet up into the car and ran a practised hand up and down each of her legs, from ankle to mid-thigh. She was too surprised to react, too confined to run.

'Don't—don't do that!' she gasped as his hand flipped her skirt up a little higher. Her legs were automatically responding now, pushing her back against the seat.

'Don't! You're not a doctor, are you?'

'Me? No, just a friend,' he chuckled. He leaned over farther and kissed her cheek. Anger overcame fear, and she pushed his hand away. 'Don't!' she half-screamed, her voice laden with tension. 'Get your hands off me! Just because you knocked me down it doesn't entitle you to a free—'

'No, of course not,' he said. He straightened slightly, flipped her skirt down, and tucked it modestly around her legs below the knees. 'Okay, Miss Modesty,' he snapped. 'If you want to bleed to death, be my guest. We'll just sit here awhile and see how much blood trickles down your leg, shall we?'

'Oh no!' she groaned. 'No!' She grabbed at the hem of her skirt and rucked it up to her waist, bending over to inspect for damage. Everything was on view, all the way up to her tiny pink bikini briefs. 'Why, it isn't bleeding at all!' she exclaimed. She squirmed farther away from him and managed to cover herself. There was a gleam in those dark eyes of his. 'If you think that was funny—!' she stammered.

'No, but it was nice,' he chuckled. 'I like pink—on good-looking girls, of course. So you're not bleeding, and the crowd has gone, but you've got a few fine bruises. Do you intend to sue me?'

On good-looking girls? Then he obviously wasn't talking about her, she knew. You learn quickly, growing up as an orphan, in the care of the state of Ohio. Cute little girls get adopted, even beyond the age of six. Homely little girls just bounce around from foster-home to foster-home. Some become brash, hard. Others, like Evelyn Hart, learn to quietly keep out of the way of life in order to survive. And the Ugly Duckling story, she knew, was merely a fairytale. Sue him? The idea startled her. Another thing that homely orphan girls learn quickly is to keep away from the law!

'You—why would I want to sue you?' she asked. 'Don't be silly. I hit you, you didn't hit me. And I thank you very much.' Another lesson from the past. Say please and thank you even if it hurts—as now. I thank you for knocking me down in the street and embarrassing me, and putting your hands on me! 'If you don't mind, my *publico* will be along any minute now.'

'The least I can do is drive you to where you're going,' he suggested. 'Why should you ride a bus when my car is already here? And air-conditioned, at that. Just how far do you have to go?'

'Only a few miles,' she gabbled, and then stopped up her mouth. Do I really want to ride with him? she asked herself. What do I know about him except that he looks—nice—and has an air-conditioned car? Bogeyman rule number one—never let a strange man get you alone someplace. Never. But the *publico* will rattle and bang and wander, and break your bones. The village where she lived was tiny, almost abandoned, and the rickety old bus that served it was more so. And air-conditioned? It was almost the end of February, the rainy season was ending, and the normal ocean breeze that regularly cooled the island was bringing in humid air. She was dressed as lightly as decency would allow—a plain white linen skirt, a lightweight V-neck blouse, those unmentionable pink briefs, and nothing else. But even at that the perspiration dripped down her forehead, down her neck, and she could feel her whole body—oozing! For the second time in ten minutes modesty and fear lost another battle. 'I live in the Playa de Santiago,' she said, 'just a few miles down the road.' She tugged at her blouse, which was developing the tendency to cling to the outlines of her delightfully full breasts.

'I know the Playa,' he said, his eyes glued to the outline her blouse could not hide. 'When we were younger my father brought us down to the island at least once a year to visit Monkey Island. Hop in, while I collect your things together.' He turned away from her and began to pick up her scattered briefcase and handbag.

'I hope there's nothing breakable in your case,' he noted as he dropped it into the back seat. 'It looks as if somebody stepped on it. A whole bunch of somebodies.'

As he climbed into the driver's seat Evy squirmed around to examine the case. The lock had not sprung, thank the Lord. Nothing held greater value for her than the signed receipts and the legal releases it contained.

'Something valuable in the case?' he asked casually as he started up the motor. The air-conditioner instantly swung into action, spraying her with dry coolness, and she spread her legs slightly to allow the greatest possible circulation.

'Yes,' she answered softly, keeping her eyes turned away from him. 'Not in money terms. They're bills—receipted bills. This is a sort of celebration for me—burn the mortgage, that sort of thing.' Receipted bills. Two years she had slaved to pay off the mass of bills that Frank had left behind, unpaid. Don Alfonso, her lawyer, had called her on Saturday to tell her that the papers had arrived. She had come up from the tiny village to Santiago on Sunday because she was eager to hold them in her own hands!

He started to shift the car into gear, then thought better of it. 'By the name of Brown,' he introduced himself. 'Jason Brown.' Evy barely touched his outstretched hand, then snatched her own back again. 'My friends call me Jase,' he added.

'You don't sound Puerto Rican, Mr Brown,' she said. 'Texas?'

'Yes, ma'am,' he laughed. 'Born in Puerto Rico, raised in the Heart of Texas. Gatesville, that is.'

'I—I'm Evelyn Hart,' she said hesitantly, still not sure

of herself, or of this stranger. Evelyn Hart. She had long since dropped the Santuccio. She hadn't used it since the day of the accident, for that matter. But it would be better to be sure, with Mr Jason Brown of Texas. It's better to set up the barriers early than too late. She fumbled with her wedding ring, to call it to his attention. He noticed. He seemed to be the type that notices everything. 'Mrs Evelyn Hart,' she added.

'Yes, of course. Mrs Evelyn Hart.' He laughed as he pushed the automatic drive lever into 'D' and started them down the wandering highway. 'And you don't much look like a Puerto Rican,' he remarked, reaching over to run a finger through her long blonde hair. She blushed, and moved sharply away from him, so far away that the door hand dug into her side. Her sun-hat was on the floor under her feet. She rescued it and began stuffing her hair back into its shelter. 'Sensitive little thing, aren't you?' he observed.

'I—I just like my privacy,' she stammered. 'I—I've been—ill for a long time. I'm not accustomed to the social graces.'

He took the corners of the old winding two-lane mountain road as if he were familiar with it. The big car hummed, the air-conditioner swished, and it was all very pleasant. Just so long as he requires two hands on the steering wheel, Evy told herself fiercely. If he makes one single move to stop on the side of the road, I'll be gone! She glued her eyes to the scenery, where the coconut palms, the plane trees, the avocado trees, all signalled that they were approaching the sea. Brilliant orange flowers of the almost odourless flamboyant tree speckled the roadside. Most of the open farm areas looked as if they were abandoned.

'You're supposed to talk, to entertain me,' Jason Brown suggested.

'Oh—well, I've not been here long,' she said. 'You

mentioned a place called Monkey Island?'

He flashed her a smile before turning back to the road. 'Just outside the port,' he commented. 'You know that the Playa de Santiago was originally the harbour for Santiago city, back in the days when coastal steamers from St Croix made stops along the east coast? There's a tiny island out in the bay, just inside the reef, called Isla de Santiago. Back in World War II when the Germans were interrupting the sea-lanes to India, a colony of Rhesus monkeys was established on that island. They're used for medical experiments. Some of the monkeys are still there, under the control of the School of Tropical Medicine. You ought to get your husband to take you out there for a visit—you'd love it. The monkeys are neither tame nor caged. They roam the island to their hearts' content, and occasionally put up with people, when they feel like it.

He turned to her, expecting some sort of answer, and she could feel herself being walled in, boxed in a corner. It was not that she hated to lie; that is another adage orphans learn early in life. 'Truth is like a pearl of great price. Use it sparingly!' But this particular man seemed to exude an aura of confidence and trust, so she decided to take a chance. 'I'm sure it would be nice,' she murmured, 'but I don't have a husband, Mr Brown. I'm a widow.'

'A widow?' He peered at her in astonishment. 'Why, you don't look to be more than nineteen. And a widow?'

'Yes,' she sighed. 'He died two years ago. And I'm twenty, actually.'

'Now I *am* sorry,' he said quietly. 'I'm sure he would be hard to replace.'

Yes, she thought immediately, impossible to replace! A girl only needs one lesson like that one to last her a lifetime! Her thoughts were pulled relentlessly back to that day in Cleveland. They had been married for three months, and separated for six, when he had appeared without warning at the house. 'I've been—away,' he laughed as he forced himself past her at the front door. His normally tanned skin was white and puffy. He wanted to rummage in the attic, he said. She refused to let him, so he knocked her down with a backhand swing to the jaw, and broke into the attic anyway. But he hadn't found what he was looking for. He came back downstairs to where she was still lying on the floor, kicked her viciously, and left. Evy had managed to pull herself up to the window as he climbed into his little red sports car. The tyres had squirted gravel as he gunned it down the short drive, but he had failed to make the turn at the bottom of the drive, and had gone crashing into the stone wall on the other side of the street.

The crash that crumpled the machine had been but a dull thud. The fire that bloomed over the wreckage had burned like the wrath of God. When the policemen had come up the walk to tell her, she was laughing, a hysterical screaming laugh that could not be shut off until after she had spent three months in the Psychiatric Pavilion of the Ohio State Hospital.

'You're crying,' Jason Brown said softly. 'Here.' He passed her an immaculate white handkerchief. She dabbed at her eyes, and knew what he was thinking. Poor little widow, barely a child, weeping for her lost love! If only he knew the truth! Well, let him think what he wanted!

After a moment she sniffled, blew her nose, and tried another tack. 'And what do you do, Mr Brown?'

'Call me Jase,' he repeated. 'I travel for the family corporation. We own a few things here and there, including a coffee *finca* up the side of the mountain there, near Rio Blanco. Know anything about coffee?'

'Oh yes,' she teased. 'I drink four or five cups every

day. I suppose you have to know more than that?'

'Somewhat more,' he returned, 'but not much. Most of our holdings are in oil. This *finca* is a sideline handed down by my grandfather. It's been losing money for the last ten years, and the Brown Corporation just doesn't like the sound of those words. So here I am, to either kill or cure it, and I'm not sure which at the moment.'

'Why, that sounds—won't that put a lot of people out of work?'

'I can't tell yet,' he said. 'That's Puerto Rico's biggest problem.' She looked at him curiously. 'How to match an American style economy into a Caribbean background. Some time when we've nothing else to do we can talk about that.'

Evy turned away so he could not read her expression. He talked as if he expected them to have a long and fruitful friendship! Which was not entirely her idea of things at all. One ride down the mountainside, yes. But certainly there was no need for anything more? She pursed her lips and shook her head in denial.

'Ah, there's the Playa,' he said. 'Which way?'

'Straight ahead,' she pointed. 'That white-walled house just up from the beach.'

'That's the old Customs House,' he exclaimed. 'You live there?'

'Yes. It was available cheap, and I had a little fix-up money, so I took it. Have you ever seen the inside?' There, I've done it, she snapped at herself, almost biting her tongue. Now I've practically invited him in. And then there'll be coffee, and then—what have I done?

'No—lord, no,' he answered. 'The Customs House was closed in our day. It looks like the Alamo, doesn't it?'

'The what?'

'Oh dear, girl, where were you educated? In the state of Texas you'd be horsewhipped for that! The Alamo was the old stone fort at San Antonio where a handful of Texas soldiers stood off the entire Mexican army, until they were wiped out to the last man. Your house looks like that—a fortress. A high wall all around everything. Barred windows, and I do believe there's a look-out port over the front door. Fit to stand off pirates, I'll bet!'

Evy looked at him quizzically. She had not really known many men in her life. None of her seven foster-fathers had ever made an impression on her, and outside of Frank, who was not the kind of person to use as a yardstick, she had no way to measure men. Acquaintances, yes. Friends, no! She blamed it on the fact that she was no raving beauty. Although her five and a half foot frame was very well endowed, it was topped by a face that could only be called Plain Jane—square, un-compromising, fluffed with baby fat, punctured by two dimples that were so deep they looked like wells. Well, that was the way she *did* look. Frank always said he had to take a plain brown paper bag to put over her head on dates! And since the day of the accident she had avoided looking at herself at all. Oh well. Here was a specimen of man she could assess. The closer they got to her home, the more he looked like a little boy who would have loved to see pirates sail up the bay while he defended the barricades!

'It's different from the inside,' she replied at last. 'It's a typical Latin-American house. It looks inward, and turns its back on the streets.' The car pulled up on a small paved area just in front of the main gate of the house. 'There's something wrong,' she told him in a tense voice, even before the vehicle came to a halt.

'What?'

'That's Doña Maria, my—my *dueña*!' The figure of her short stout and elderly woman was huddled against the wall of the house, hands covering her face as she rocked back and forth.

'Doña?' he queried as he unlatched his door.

'It's not used in reference to nobility,' she snapped, struggling to free herself from her seat-belt. 'There is no pride of nobility in Puerto Rico. It's a title used as a sign of respect for older people, or those who have accomplished great things. Should I call her my housekeeper? She's kind and lovable and seventy, so I call her Doña and we both do the housework!'

'But you also called her your *dueña*?'

'Well, of course. I'm a widow, but too young to live alone. It's the island custom to have a *dueña*. Why shouldn't I conform to a very enjoyable custom?'

Now that they were both out of the car it was a matter of only a few steps to the side of the woman whose black dress was so startlingly silhouetted against the whitewashed wall. The woman lifted her head as they came up to her, and waved towards the door. '*Madre de Dios!*' she quavered. 'I am gone to my sister's house for only an hour, and look what happens! Inside. *Paracer que guerra!*'

'Now, now,' comforted Evy, folding the tiny figure in her arms.

'No! Look,' the woman insisted. 'Look inside.'

'Okay, stop crying,' Evy insisted more firmly. 'Mr—Jason—would you mind coming in with me?' She stopped short. Why tell him that you're petrified? Why tell him that you shy from shadows? He probably knows that anyway! She took a deep breath, and managed the two steps to the front door. The protective grille had been swung back out of the way, and she tested the knob. The door was unlocked. Gently she pushed it open, and stepped back. 'I—I had an experience in Cleveland once,' she told him over her shoulder. 'I came home and a burglar was still inside. I—I' Her voice ground to a halt.

'Don't worry,' he said as he brushed by her. 'If there's

a burglar in there, I'll rout him out. Wait here.' He pushed her back against the wall, not too gently. Lordy, I'll have to call this black and blue Sunday, she told herself as she fingered the new bruise on her upper arm. He was gone for almost five minutes, and then reappeared.

'Well, somebody's been here,' he told her, 'but he or they have gone. I couldn't find a soul.'

Evy started towards the door, only to be bypassed by Doña Maria. Now that a man was in control of the scene, Maria was prepared to battle with dragons. Evy followed them into the house, more than willing to let the brave precede her.

A tiny hallway gave entrance to a large living room on the left hand, and two steps leading downwards into the garden, on the right. The heady scent of honeysuckle flooded the area, tinted with jasmine, and a few other blended odours. From the branches of the mimosa tree in the back of the tiny enclosed garden a pair of brilliant parakeets screeched a welcome.

Evy paused to let the beauty of it all work to restore her spirit, then turned into the living room. 'Oh, my heaven!' she moaned as she crossed the threshold. The room was furnished in bamboo and wickerwork. All the chairs were upturned, their cushions slashed open, their stuffing pulled out and scattered across the polished floor. The doors of all the glass-fronted cabinets along the wall hung open. Both her well-loved Dresden figurines lay smashed on the floor. Nothing remained as it had been only hours before, a quiet, restful, high-ceilinged retreat.

She knew what had happened. It had happened before—twice in Cleveland, once in Chicago, and now here. 'Oh God,' she moaned, slipping to her knees on the floor. 'Why do they have to keep terrorising me? What do they want? What have I done to deserve all this!' She was close to breakdown, and Jase knew it. He motioned Maria into the kitchen for water, then came over and helped Evy to her feet, drawing her close against him. Her head fitted very neatly under his chin. Very comfortable, he noticed, brushing down the cloud of blonde hair that was still twirling around her head. Evy sobbed on his shirtfront uncontrollably. He walked her back to the steps that led to the garden. It took half an hour to soothe her back to sensibility.

She rested against him after the storm had passed, then was struck by a terrible thought, and pulled away from him anxiously. 'My workroom!' she exclaimed. She was away from him like an Olympic sprinter, running down the little hall to the room at the back of the house. This corner room was bathed in light. Two windows opened in the back wall, two on the side, and the entire inner wall was a series of louvred shutters that opened on the garden. Papers were strewn across the floor, and the drawers of four filing cabinets stood open. But the big drawing board in the middle of the room had been left standing, unmolested.

'What in the world is this?' he asked as he came up behind her.

'My workroom,' she sighed. 'There are two weeks' work on that one drawing sheet.'

'Cartoons?' His eyebrows elevated slightly.

'Go ahead and sneer,' she muttered under her breath. 'It's a living!'

'You draw cartoons for somebody?' he asked.

'I draw cartoons for me,' she said sarcastically. 'It's hard work, but my panel is syndicated in sixty-two newspapers now. I don't suppose you've ever read the cartoon page?'

'I don't suppose,' he laughed. 'Not since I was fourteen. But it's a living?'

'Yes,' she sighed, 'it's a living—at least now it is. Not

before. When I was just starting out, three years ago, it was an ego exercise. But after, when I met Belle Samples of World-Wide Syndicate, it began to pay. And now it supports me, pays the bills, and leaves a little bit left over. What a mess!'

'Anything missing?' he asked.

For some reason he had touched on a sore spot. 'How in the world would I know?' she snarled. 'I just got here!'

'Hey, don't yell at me,' he returned. 'I'm the guy who ran you down with my car, not the burglar. They were looking for something specific. Did they find it, I wonder?'

'I don't know!' Evy was on the verge of crying again. She righted the workroom stool and slumped on to it, all her ration of courage for the day used up. 'I—I just don't know what to do,' she whispered, and then the tears came. Maria was a great help. She edged her way into the room, watched Evy's tears begin, and joined her with some of her own.

Jason wavered between the two of them, not knowing which one needed comfort the most. Finally he decided. He walked over to Evy and pulled her against his hip, making soft comforting noises and running his fingers through her hair. She responded by snuggling closer to him. 'Do you want me to do something about all this?' he asked softly.

'Yes,' she pleaded, still sniffling. 'May I have your handkerchief?'

He smiled down at her, a friendly compassionate smile, and perhaps something more; she could not see because her hair had swung forward over her face again. He patted her head gently, then went in search of a telephone.

Twenty minutes later he had talked to the duty officer in the Insular Police District office, and organised a partial clean-up in the kitchen. 'They're sending a man over right away,' he told her. 'The Playa is too small to have an officer stationed here all the time. And in the meantime, if we could get the kitchen cleaned up, a couple of good cups of coffee are indicated.' He made some vague move towards picking things up, and the two women swept him out of the way with calm efficiency.

The coffee was hot, and Puerto Rican. Stronger than anything available on supermarket shelves, it was brewed into a thick heavy drink, and then made into an extract, before being mixed, black and wicked, half a cup, with the other half filled with hot milk. They sat around the resurrected table and sipped. '*Café con leche*,' sighed Jase. 'After all my years with coffee and chicory mixed, this stuff is a marvellous change. So, you're a cartoonist?' She nodded. 'Where in the world do you get all those ideas?'

'It's not hard,' she said. 'My strip only appears in the Sunday papers. I need four frames per week. In an ordinary full working day I can turn out sixteen frames. They just come—the ideas, I mean. Although that filing cabinet is loaded with thoughts I haven't used yet, just in case I run dry. I set up the strip, write the plot, draw the principal characters, pen the dialogue down below, and mail it all to Chicago. They have artists there who fill in the colour and backgrounds, put the dialogue in the balloons, and send it to the printer. I generally keep four months ahead of the deadline. It's the only way I can keep my sanity.'

'You're very nervous, aren't you, for all that assurance?' he commented; and Evy looked up from her cup to find his dark eyes boring into her. What have I said now? she asked herself. I'm fairly presentable, even though my hair is a mess. My dress is relatively clean. He can't know that I don't wear anything under it. Or can he? She suddenly had the feeling that he was reading her mind. His eyes dropped down to where her breasts were straining against the material of her blouse, and she blushed, shifted herself in her seat, and turned away from him.

They sat in silence for another five minutes, nursing their coffee. The sound of a police siren drifted in to them, and a car squealed to a stop in front of the house. Jason went out to the door. Maria began to bustle, making more coffee, and Evy froze in her chair. Policemen always represented a problem to her. She could not forget that black night when Frank had burned in his car. And the times that followed, before she fled from Cleveland in almost total hysteria. And it was always a policeman who was the catalyst!

'Mrs Hart,' Jason said formally, so unlike the man he had been in Santiago, 'may I present a friend of mine, Sergeant Velasquez, of the District detective squad.'

'*Con mucho gusto*,' Evy said automatically. He was short and wiry, this policeman—swarthy, with a mop of raven black hair. He was not in uniform. He wore tan slacks, and an aloha shirt sparkling with reds and greens and yellows. He looked young. He pulled out a chair and sat down at the table. Maria came over from the stove, looked at him, and rattled off a long command in rapid Spanish, and the policeman blushed. '*Si*, Abuela,' he said. Maria poured his coffee and left the room.

'Ah, *señora*,' he sighed. 'It is *muy caliente*, no?' He hauled a huge bandana from his back pocket and wiped the perspiration from his face. Evy acknowledged with a nod.

He shook his head. 'My grandmother will be disappointed,' he sighed. 'She demands that I solve the case this afternoon, because the Señora wants to go to the beach tomorrow.'

'Your grandmother?' laughed Evy. 'Doña Maria is your grandmother?'

'Just so,' he laughed back at her. 'And me, I am a

great disappointment to her, you understand. Thirty years old, and I am only a sergeant, no?'

He put both hands on the table, palms down, and looked around the room. Evy could almost see his brain clicking. Sugar container, opened and dumped. Flour container, upside down. Dishes strewn across the floor, some smashed. Garbage can, overturned and empty. He pulled out a notebook and began to pencil in entries in a tiny well-formed hand.

'Now, *señora*,' he said, 'you have not lived here long?'

'Just one month to the day,' she said softly.

'And you came here from—?'

'Chicago—and Cleveland, Ohio. I'd lived in Cleveland all my life, almost.'

'And I understand you are a widow?'

'Yes,' she sighed, and started to amplify, but stopped. 'Yes,' she repeated.

He scribbled a few notes in his book, then thumped the end of his pen on the table. 'My men examine the other rooms,' he continued. 'But this is curious. You have no idea who did this? What they could be looking for?'

'No,' she stammered, 'I—I have no idea. I don't think anything is missing, but why would somebody vandalise my home? Why?' The tears were threatening again. Jason came around the table to stand behind her, pulling her back against him, treasuring her hands. She fought off the tears. 'You must excuse me,' she sighed. 'I—I've been ill, and I—'

'*No importa*,' the detective said. 'It is enough to make you nervous, this. Now, let me understand. You have had this happen to you before, this—vandalising?'

'Yes,' she confessed. 'After my husband—died. I went to a hospital for a time. When I got—when I was released, I came home and found everything in the house just like this. I think they must have spent days at

it. Everything was torn apart except my Christmas orna-
ments in the attic. Everything.'

'And you called the police?'

'Yes, but they found nothing. I cleaned up the place,
and then, a month later, I had to—had to go back to the
hospital for a—for a check-up. And it happened again!
The police said—they said—it must be someone with a
personal grudge and that I—because of Frank—that I
ought to leave town.'

'This is your husband, this Frank?'

'Yes, my husband. So I left Cleveland. I put all my
heavy things in storage, and went to Chicago. I stayed at
a residential hotel there, getting my affairs with the
World-Wide Syndicate in order. And at the end of the
first week, somebody—'

'Came in and tore your room all apart?'

'Yes!' She spread her hands out towards him in a
gesture of appeal, then dropped them in her lap. Her
head bent forward, masking her tortured face.

'And you called the police in Chicago?'

'No—I was too scared. I had a little money, so I just
packed up and ran. I picked Puerto Rico because it was
far away, and still a part of the United States. And I told
the real estate man in San Juan that I wanted a small
house in the smallest village the farthest removed from
any place else he knew. He sent me to Playa de Santiago.
I just ran—like a damn rabbit!' Her indignation was
turned against herself. You haven't an ounce of spirit,
have you? she demanded of herself. Not an ounce!
Damn rabbit. You deserve everything you get.

She looked up, flushed, and surprised a look of
admiration in the eyes of both the men. She had not
noticed, in the past two years, that illness and care had
worn away the baby fat on her cheeks, lengthened the
line of her jaw, and turned her face into a thing of
haunted beauty.

'And when you ran, *señora*, you carried nothing with you?'

'Nothing? I came with a suitcase, if that's what you mean. But when I found this place, I sent back to Valley Movers, in Cleveland, and they packed and crated everything from Cleveland and Chicago too, and shipped it down. Everything, mind you. I had some bagged garbage in the kitchen can in Chicago. They packed it all and sent the whole thing. Lord, did it smell!' She laughed, but it was a high hysterical laugh. 'They even shipped me my garbage!'

'And when did all these goods arrive?'

'A week ago?' she turned to Maria for confirmation. 'Yes, a week ago.'

The detective tapped his pencil on the table and looked over his notes. Evy could see that there was some eye communication between the detective and Jason Brown. They nodded at each other over her head, as if they had reached a solution to the problem.

'But they are very quick,' the sergeant mused.

'It's a big business,' Jason returned. 'They have plenty of people on the island.'

'You mean because of the gambling casinos? It is the official position of the government that there are no underworld connections involved in Puerto Rico's gambling concessions.' The detective had a very small smile playing at the corners of his mouth.

'No, of course not,' agreed Jason. 'As soon as Castro shut down the mob in Havana, gambling opened here in Puerto Rico. But, as you say, there is no connection.'

'Not anywhere,' the sergeant concluded glumly. 'Now, *señora*, what is it that your husband did for a living in Cleveland?' Evy hesitated, biting down on her lower lip. Frank had never wanted her to know, but it had taken only one party with his 'friends' for her to discover what was going on, and then it took careful acting to conceal from him that she knew. She shuddered at the thought.

'I—I don't know,' she sighed. 'He said it was importing and exporting, but he never told me the name of the company. We were only married for a short time.'

'Yes, of course. And it was an extended honeymoon, so you would not enquire too closely, no?'

She looked him straight in the eye without flinching, but without answering either. Let him think what he wants, she told herself fiercely. Certainly it was three months of honeymooning. Not counting the two separate times when he put me in the hospital! Her fingers automatically caressed the line of her jaw, where a barely visible bump still reminded her. Let him think what he wants!

The detective harrumphed, tapped his pen, then folded everything into his pocket. He was slow to stand up, and again there was some sort of unspoken agreement between the two men.

'It will be some time,' he told her. 'We will talk to the people, you understand. It is a small village, the Playa. Someone might have seen something. And then we will contact the Cleveland police. But, *señora*, I would not like to think of you alone here overnight. We cannot afford policemen to guard you at this moment. It would be well if—you have friends?'

'Of course she has,' Jason interrupted. 'Me. She can come to the *finca* with me. And Maria too, of course!'

'I—I've imposed on you too much already,' Evy said stiffly. In the back of her mind there was a raging argument going on, a fight between the undeniable attraction of Jason's personality, and the older fears that haunted her. In her heart she knew she wanted to go—go with him, that was. This home, this loving place, had suddenly become a dark threatening cave!

'Nonsense,' he said, and she took a deep, relieved

breath. 'Pack up a few things. Enough for a week, perhaps. And we'll keep in touch with Ramón by telephone.'

'Ramón?'

'Sergeant Velasquez,' he laughed. 'Ramón and I go a long way back.'

'Will everything be safe here?' she asked the policeman. 'Will they come back and—'

'If they come back we will have some arrangement,' the detective said. 'Take whatever you want from here, no? If they missed what they are looking for, they will come again. And it would be better if they do not find you here. *Comprendo?*'

'Yes, I understand. Thank you—Ramón.'

'*De nada, señora.*' She held out her hand to him, and he took it, smiling. I don't believe it, she thought, almost panicking. He's going to kiss my hand! And he did.

As they turned away from the door she noticed that the afternoon was creeping away, and a band of gold rimmed the restless sea at her doorstep. And at least something had regained courage. The pair of parakeets who lived in the garden had begun to chirp away, practising for evensong.

'Doña Maria,' called Jason, 'will you pack the clothes that you and the Señora will need, *por favor?*' The elderly woman smiled widely over two gold teeth and bustled away.

'And what do I do?' Evy asked him primly.

'You just stand still,' he laughed. 'If Ramón can kiss you then so can I.' And he did, but not on her hand.

CHAPTER 2

IT was not until Evy had been in her room for several minutes that she came to her senses. What was it that had caused such a reaction? Jason was a companionable man, calm in crisis, friendly. When he kissed her she had struggled like a tiger-cat to break free from him. Something had seized her, broken the calm exterior she had maintained for months. When first his arms came around her she had stood silently, meaning to offer him a passive response as payment for his kindness, but the moment his lips touched hers, so had panic. Her two tiny hands had beat against him, like a moth fluttering at a flame. And when he had increased the pressure she had become a mindless thing.

Her left hand broke free from his prison and slashed at his face, raking a bloodstained furrow of fingernails down his cheek. He released her, and she staggered down the corridor and slammed her bedroom door behind her. And now, sitting on the edge of her bed, she wondered why. She held her sharp-clawed fingers up before her and asked herself over and over again, why?

Certainly he knew by now that she frightened easily. But surely not as easily as this? For a moment she seemed to hear Doctor Pheizer, just before she left the hospital. 'Don't bury things. Get them out in the open. And fight!' Was that what she was, a woman without courage? It was hard, in her bewildered mind, to separate truth from fiction. What was the truth? Since that day in Cleveland she had lost all her courage. She was frightened by anything that moved, that seemed authoritative, that seemed—too masculine!

That was *his* trouble. He was all male, too overpoweringly male. But she knew she had to fight her fears, or give in entirely to them. In the back of her mind an unwanted picture formed. Rows of women, sitting in total withdrawal from the world, their faces changing with their dreams, but living a dream life, catatonic. And that, she knew, was what happened to people who gave in to their fears. She knew that she had just enough strength left to hate the idea. Fight back, that was the only answer. And here to hand was a—target? Partner? Well, at least a friend! And that was the moment that Evelyn Hart committed herself to live and work and share with Jason Brown. If he was still waiting for her. If he had not already given her up as a weepy shrew, not worth waiting for.

She struggled into her lightweight pantsuit, knowing that although the tropical day had been warm, the night would quickly cool down under the influence of offshore breezes. She dressed carefully, as if she *would* be going to the top of the mountain. As if he were still waiting. What a fool she had been! She brushed her hair, leaving it loosely tied at the nape of her neck with a dark ribbon. Then she worked up her courage, opened the door, and walked down the hall.

'The Señor, he waits at the door,' Maria told her. 'He has the bags taken in the car, no? You are tired, *linda*. The day is too long.'

'He is—angry? *Irritado?*'

'Ah no, *linda*. But he has cut himself, and he wishes to stop the bleeding. *Vamonos!*'

Maria bustled out to the front door, with Evy lagging behind. She could hear them both laughing as she came around the corner. He certainly didn't *sound* angry. What could the pair of them be up to? She found out quickly enough. Maria was holding up a little black rag doll, while Jason was doing his best to tie it up by a string, so that it hung in the middle of the doorway.

'What in the world are you doing?' asked Evy. Maria turned towards her with an apprehensive look on her face. 'It is the *resguardo*,' she explained hurriedly. 'The—what you say—guardian? Nothing can pass it with evil in the heart, no?'

'Superstition,' Evy snorted.

'Ju-ju,' responded Jason. 'Haiti's not that far away, and there's more than a little respect for an Obeah man around here. It can't hurt, you know.'

'I have to take it away?' Maria pleaded.

'No,' returned Evy, mollified. 'As you say, it can't hurt.'

'You go to the car, Maria,' he said. 'I have something private I have to say to Mrs Hart.' The little duenna smiled. Vandals and robbers she did not understand, but the way of a man with a woman, that she understood very well. And like any knowledgeable *dueña*, she walked away. After all, it is the purpose of a duenna to smooth the path to the altar, not to recruit for a nunnery!

'I—I want to apologise.' Evy hastened to get her statement made before Jason's wrath overwhelmed her. 'I shouldn't have done that. Never!' But there was no flash of anger in return. 'I've cut your cheek,' she said tenderly, reaching out to trace a path down his cheek beside the scratches. 'I'll get some peroxide. Or would you prefer antibiotic cream?'

'You don't have rabies,' he chuckled. 'Peroxide will do. And you needn't apologise—I should have kept my hands to myself. Please accept *my* apology. I'm sorry, Mrs Hart. Friends?'

'I—of course,' muttered Evy as she hurried away to the bathroom for peroxide and pads. So she had *not* turned him off! And while he was making an apology his face had lit with an infectious grin, like the one he had worn when taking about pirates. She had caught the infection and smiled back. But hers was a creaky one-sided smile. Not bad, considering that she had little or nothing to smile about in the previous years, but still something that needed improvement.

Fifteen minutes later they crowded into the front seat of Jason's big car, moving back up the mountain road towards Santiago on the same highway they had recently come down. He ushered her into the front seat, then established Maria on the same seat with her, even though the entire back of the car was empty. When he slid into the driver's seat his muscular thigh pressed against hers, and as he drove his right hand would occasionally slide across the inches between them to rest for brief seconds on her knee. He looked impassively up the road. Evy looked impassive too, but it was all a lie. Deep inside, something was churning, growing, encompassing her. Every time his hand rested feather-light on her knee chills chased up her spine, but her new resolve gave her the strength not to reject him.

Despite the coolness of the air-conditioning, tiny beads of perspiration glistened on her forehead. It's really a basic emotion, she lectured herself. It's called lust, a very simply animal reaction, and I'm as much of an animal as he is. We'll go to his farm, and we'll fence with each other for a time, and then he'll invite me to go to bed with him. And if I can find the nerve, I'll do it! Then the whole affair will pass over, and I'll be a better woman for it. If I can find the nerve. I wonder what *he* feels?

He started to whistle as they wound up the mountain road. 'My *finca* is only five miles from your home,' he told her, 'straight up the side of the mountain. But there aren't any roads that go straight up, so we have to go around the sides of a square to get there. Well, look what's here!' They had arrived back where they had started, at the central plaza of Santiago de Puerto Rico, but there was one big difference.

At one o'clock the square had been empty, the town asleep. Now, in the coolness of the late afternoon, the area was crowded. Women, in gaily dressed groups of two or three, were strolling arm in arm clockwise around the square. Young women. Outside of the circle the women made was another, all men, strolling in groups of two or three, counter-clockwise. Jason brought the car to a halt.

'Is the *paseo*,' Maria explained. 'Every Sunday afternoon, no? All the girls of the age for marriage, they stroll in the Plaza for an hour. The *dueñas*, they sit on the benches around the fountain to watch. And if a boy sees a girl who attracts him, he asks among the men for her name. Then his family contacts her family—and if there is no objection, the courtship begins. My grandson Enrique says that in New York they have businesses, marriage bureaux, but this is much better. It is the old custom. Customs become old because they work, you understand.' And with that bit of wisdom she settled back in her seat again.

'Did you ever promenade in the *paseo*?' Evy asked Maria.

The old lady cackled. 'Many and many a day,' she laughed. 'When I was young I was like you, *linda*, but our family had no money, so I promenaded for many a Sunday. Not here, you understand. Fajardo is my— what to say—home town?'

'And what happens to the girl who never attracts a suitor?'

'Ah well, it happens,' the old lady sighed. 'Old customs do not guarantee happiness, just continuity. In the old days such a one would perhaps retire to the church, or be a "maiden aunt" to her family. Nowadays they go into the factories, no? Much has changed, and I am not sure that I like it. *Ay Dios mio!*'

'You want to stop and join the *paseo*?' Jason asked Evy. His mouth was smiling, but his eyes were not. They watched her like a hawk, gleaming, piercing. She tried to make light of it all.

'No,' she returned. 'I've had my chance. One should never expect a second time around.'

Whatever it was he said, it was under his breath. But she was almost certain that he muttered, 'The hell you say!' In any event, it gave her a strange little glow of happiness that lasted throughout the rest of the trip.

They were beginning to climb sharply now, on an unpaved but well-kept farm-to-market road. Jason cut the air-conditioners and opened the automatic windows. The breeze flooded the car with the cloyingness of the red jasmine, the overwhelming ginger odour of the frangipani, and the evensong of the *coqui*. They turned off the road on to an uphill dirt track, bending back and forth in its serpentine assault on the mountain, crossing the same stream six times before they came to a halt in a paved courtyard.

Twilight had turned quickly into tropical night, illuminated only by brilliant stars, and a slice of the full moon, just hanging over the shoulder of El Yunque Mountain. Buildings loomed in every direction around them, their full shapes and forms concealed by the shadows of clustered trees. Another flood of scent swept into the car. Lemon, sharp and penetrating. Orange, fresh from the blossom. Roses, in serried ranks and odours in a formal garden. And over it all the sharp fragrance of the little white coffee blossoms.

'Welcome to El Semillo,' said Jason.

'What's that mean?'

'El Semillo? That's Spanish for "the seed", he replied. They left the car at the garage, and walked up a pebbled path between the rose garden and the dark shadow of warehouse buildings. They were upon the house before Evy realised. It was a huge wooden frame structure, set up off the ground on creosote pilings, and tucked away among tall swaying trees. 'It was built on stilts to let the breeze cool the floor,' Jason explained. 'And it also helps to keep out the creepy-crawlies. Like it?'

She took his arm and squeezed it in a show of approval. 'It's so big,' she said. 'And nothing at all like my house. Did you know that the outside walls of my house are two feet thick?'

'I said you lived in a fortress,' he chuckled. 'Now here, everything is on one elevated floor. All the rooms except the kitchen are up there on that platform. What looks to be a second floor is not. That's a completely screened porch up there. Come on in.' He took her hand in his and led the way up a set of concrete stairs to an enormous veranda, and then into a dimly lit living room, whose glass sliding doors provided and all-around view of the area. While Jason conferred with his housekeeper, Evy wandered to the other side of the room and looked down on a bustling stream and a lily pond. The smell of lemon was heavy in the air here, stamping out the lesser fragrances.

'We'll have dinner in a few minutes,' he said as he came over to her. 'Pot-luck, of course. You don't object to Puerto Rican food?'

'How could I?' she laughed. 'Maria does all our cooking for us. But perhaps we could keep the peppers a little lighter than usual?' And the conversation, she thought. Perhaps we could keep the conversation a little lighter than usual? Why, after all these years, am I stirred by this man? When he comes close it's almost like warming myself at a fireplace. Don't get too involved, Evy. Don't get too involved. Frank was sweet enough to eat before you married him, and look what he turned into. And this man is so much bigger, so much stronger than Frank ever was!

'No problem there,' promised Jason. 'Do you really like my house?' She nodded. He took her arm again, and led her around the living room area, pointing out the dining room, the study, several bedrooms (each with its own bath), and an immense solarium. 'And the kitchen's still downstairs. You know, in the old days here they cooked on charcoal, and that required a concrete footing, and fire protection. Everything else has changed, but the kitchen is still downstairs, with a dumb waiter connecting directly to the dining room.'

'But why the fireplace?' she queried, as they paused in front of a massive stone hearth on the north side of the room.

'Hey, it's springtime now,' he chuckled. 'You should have been here in December. Rain, rain, rain—cold chilling rain, pushed along by ocean breezes. Did you know that on December the fifth the temperature up here dropped to sixty-six degrees?' She made suitable noises, not prepared to tell him how cold it was in Chicago on that day. 'And with a completely open house, that's cold,' Jason continued. 'The fireplace was my grandfather's idea. My father added all the sliding glass doors.'

'That all sounds pretty swish,' she laughed. 'Where did Maria go?'

'Missing your *dueña* so soon?' He grinned down at her. 'I swear that I will not take advantage of you, Mrs Hart. Maria has gone off with Delfinia to her cottage. She'll be staying in one of our six guest cottages, by the way. Your room is just off the living room. Want to freshen up?'

For some reason Evy felt uneasy, unsure. 'I—I would rather stay here with you,' she stammered. 'I don't—I feel unsettled.'

'Come out on the porch,' he said in a comforting tone. His hand was tucked under her arm, creating a pool of tension. 'It's hard to see anything at night,' he continued, 'but there's a treat for you in just a few minutes. Come?'

She went gladly, enjoying the sensation as his hand slipped down her forearm until it enfolded her hand, and squeezed gently. He led her out on the section of porch that overlooked the lily pond.

'Down there.' He gestured to a dark patch between the house and the stream, where trellises were darkly covered with hanging bulbous shapes. 'Watch as the moon touches them,' he ordered. She held her breath as the golden orb of the moon edged over the rooftree of the house, and its light touched the darkness. Instantly she could see the flowers, little closed pods, hanging head down in the shape of church bells. '*Campagna*,' he said quietly. 'Moon bells. Watch.'

Warily she peered into the silvery half light. As the moon caressed the pods, they began to open, releasing a heavy perfume as the pods lifted to search the sky, petals unfolding into white flowers.

'Magnificent!' she whispered. 'Magnificent! Why am I whispering? Would the noise scare them?'

'Silly!' He took her arm again. 'That other little bell ringing behind us says that dinner's ready.'

They dined on an island favourite, *aroz con pollo*. A single dish meal, it contained saffron-coloured rice, highly flavoured, with chunks of chicken intermixed. The table was of lightweight bamboo, highly polished, with a white damascene cover, and silver candles. 'This is the Puerto Rican equivalent of Irish stew,' Jason explained. 'There's always enough rice in the pot for extra visitors. And if there are any left-overs, it tastes better the second and third time around.'

'Lovely,' returned Evy, already full, and now

prepared to sip at the delicate French wine served with the meal. 'I must say that was good. Maria and I tend to have pork and rice, or beans and rice. This sort of living could grow on you.'

'I'm glad you see it that way,' he said. She looked up at him quickly. There was a predatory gleam in his eye, and a tiny smile played at the corners of his mouth. She took a larger sip of wine to cover her confusion, and almost choked herself.

Maria excused herself early, going off to chatter with Delfinia in the kitchen. Jason got up from the table and led Evy back out on to the porch. They sank into the soft luxury of a porch glider, he at one end, she at the other.

'Cognac?' he offered. 'It's easy to get.' She watched as he covered the bottom of a globe of glass in her hands. 'From the French islands, of course. For many years the Playa de Santiago was a port of entry for French wines and liqueurs from St Croix. There's many an old house hereabouts with a well stocked cellar.'

Evy sipped at the smooth warmth of the cognac, cuddling the glass between her hands. Somewhere in the back of her mind a voice was trying to sound a warning. Wine for dinner, cognac after, it kept saying. What does he really want for dessert? Me? Watch out! That had to be the password for the night. Despite all her little dreams, she was not yet ready for a relationship with a man. Not until she found out how she had poisoned her marriage with Frank.

'It must be fun to live in a place like this,' she sighed. 'Do you prefer it to Texas?'

'Yes,' he said definitely. 'Both places have their good sides and their bad, but Texas is crowded. I come from a big family. My dad still runs the works up there, and my four brothers and three sisters. There are more chiefs than Indians!'

'So you prefer to be down here running the farm?' The

idea did not match her assessment of him, and her nose wrinkled at the thought. He chuckled as he watched.

'No, I'm not trying to be a big frog in a little puddle,' he said. 'The farm is my headquarters, and a sideline. I also control everything the family owns in the Caribbean, and some things I own outright. I have a petrochemical plant here on the island. The family has a refinery in Arruba, and we share ownership in a chain of banks from Santo Domingo south through the Virgin Islands.'

'Oh,' was the only comment Evy could squeeze out. Oh! Lord, I'm way in over my head. A millionaire, give or take a few oil wells. I suppose that just makes me weekend entertainment! Well, I may never make it to this height again, so why don't I enjoy it while I'm here?

'And you're the oldest one in the family?' she hazarded.

'As it happens,' he laughed. 'How can you tell?'

'I read it once, somewhere. Oldest children grow up to be very bossy people.' She sat forward at the edge of the glider, trying to be primly proper, trying to hide the fact that her fingers were trembling too much to hold the glass.

'Oho! I take it you weren't the oldest in your family?' Jason was looking down his nose at her. It was a very imperial nose—a Roman nose indeed.

'Me? I'm the oldest and the youngest. I became an orphan when I was six months old. I never knew my parents, or if I had any brothers or sisters—or anything. The State of Ohio was kind enough to raise me in foster-homes until I was seventeen. When I graduated from high school they wished me well, gave me twenty-five dollars, and sent me out on my own. I envy you.'

'And that's why you married so young?'

'I suppose so. I was just two months past my seventeenth birthday when Frank came along. He was the swinging life I thought I wanted. I felt like a kid with a winning lottery ticket! And then he was gone and my merry-go-round broke down!'

'You must have loved him dearly,' Jason commented gently. Yes, I must have loved him dearly, her conscience shouted at her. What did I do to turn him into such a monster? It had to be my fault. It had to be! The cognac glass, wet in her nervous hands, slipped and smashed into a thousand pieces on the floor. Hold your tongue, she commanded herself. Hold your tongue. But the combination of wines and moonlight—and man—overset her controls, and she heard herself speaking, as if from a great distance.

'I hated him,' she said dully, honestly. 'I'm lucky—he killed himself before he killed me!' The hiss of his sudden intake of breath cut the air.

'You hated him?' He stood up abruptly, upsetting the balance of the swinging glider, sending her backward against the cushions.

She looked up at him, appraising the clean-cut look, the utter normality of a real man. How could he possibly understand? And yet she had the driving compulsion to *make* him understand.

'Yes,' she sighed. 'He said that I—he said—' Good God, I *can't* tell anybody what he said. I can't! She swallowed convulsively, and brushed away a forming tear. 'He said—I was not a—satisfactory wife. He started to beat me up. Out of the three months we lived together, he sent me to the hospital twice. I finally got a court order restraining him. And then I bought a double-barrelled shotgun. And that was the end of Cinderella's dream. Would you believe it?' Her voice rose to a hysterical pitch. 'He came with a truck one day when I was out, and cleared everything out of the house except my old junk in the attic. How about that? He even took back my glass slipper!'

She jumped up, quivering, prepared to run, but not knowing where. Jason came to her and enveloped her shaking figure in his strong arms. For a second she struggled against him and then gave up, resting her chin just over his heart, squeezing herself closer. Gradually the shuddering stopped, and she was quiescent.

'I don't know why I said that,' she muttered into his shirt front. 'For two years I've managed to avoid saying anything. Why now?'

'Because of the day,' he comforted her. His deep mellow voice poured balm over her tired spirit. 'Because of the dog and the burglars, and the tension, and the wine.' He ran a comforting finger through her loose hair.

And because of you, Evy told herself. Because you're warm and comforting and sympathetic—and maybe just a tiny bit because of the cognac. But mostly because of you. If only I dared to snatch at the golden ring again, I'd snatch you! But I'm not ready. Not any way near ready. If only I could have met you next year!

'Is the waterfall over?' he asked quietly.

She leaned back to look up at his face. 'Yes,' she sniffed, 'I think so. I think that all I've done today is cry—all over you, too. I think I've ruined your shirt.'

'Don't worry about it,' he said, 'I own another one.' His strong arm came around her shoulders, and he ushered her back to the front edge of the screened porch. The moonlight was silver-bright across the tiny garden. It sparkled on the moving water of the lily-pond, played among the threads of the bougainvillea vines, and glinted off the brilliant petals of the *campagna de luna*.

'Don't scar your image of life with the memories of one man,' he counselled. 'Your husband sounds like a bad movie plot. Surely other men you've dated could show you that.'

Evy half turned to bury her face in his chest again,

trying to hide her feelings. 'I only ever dated one boy before Frank,' she said, 'and nobody since. I—I think—I wish—'

'You wish what?' he encouraged.

'I wish I could turn the clock back. Could be sixteen again, with a new start in life.'

'Maybe you can,' he murmured. 'You know what I wish?'

'No. What?'

'I wish I could kiss you, without being maimed for life!'

She pushed slowly away from him, but still within the circle of his arms. His warm supporting arms. His mobile face wore a smile at the corners of his mouth, but a worry-furrow on his forehead. Kissing was not something one encountered often in state-run foster-homes. Frank was the only man who had *ever* kissed her—and his kisses were a terrible foretaste of what was to come. And yet—

'I think it could be arranged,' she said in a very small, trembling voice.

Jason leaned down to her slowly, blotting out the moonlight as his head came closer. Gently, softly, his warm moist lips touched her cheek, and then her mouth. She closed her eyes. Gradually the pressure of his lips increased. She started to break away, to say something to him, but the minute her lips parted his searching mouth shut out the world as her unpractised body and mind rose to fever levels. For endless time she hung between earth and heaven, comforted, intrigued, tantalised. When Jason gently broke the contact she hung helplessly in his arms, feet unable to support her.

'I think you'd better go to bed, Mrs Hart,' he whispered in her ear. 'Alone.' She backed away from him, too dazed to understand. As her wilful, trembling feet carried her away from him, she turned and looked over her shoulder. He was watching her with a brooding look, as if regretting that he had sent her away.

'We'll talk tomorrow,' he called after her. Evy half-waved a hand in acknowledgement, and managed to fumble her way into her bedroom.

CHAPTER THREE

Evy had expected to spend a sleepless night in a strange bed. Instead, the cool winds blew down from the mountain, fluttering her curtains, and clearing her restless mind of all her fears and nightmares. Morning struck a flame of sunlight across her windows, invading her senses with the heaviness of spring blossoms and the sound of birds. She awoke slowly, savouring the freshness of life as she had never done before. Through her window she could hear the bustle in the kitchen, the clattering of dishes, and the smell of bacon frying. In the back of her mind was a memory. A man had kissed her, and she had thoroughly enjoyed it! She smiled as she struggled out from under the light sheet that covered her, and padded into the bathroom.

She dressed casually—white cord slacks, and a loose hand-embroidered blouse, buttoned down the front. Her hair was a daily ritual. Ten minutes of brushing, then another ten minutes to braid it up and pin it in a coronet on top of her head. It was almost a religious ceremony, instituted by the therapist at the hospital as a form of meditation. Its steady repetitious requirements always seemed to soothe her nerves—as it did today.

But her stomach kept sending up distress signals, so she shortened her meditaton, pinned her hair up loosely, and wandered out into the corridor. A pair of voices sounded in the distance. She followed the sound—and her nose—out through the living room. The delightful sound of chimes led her to the open front window that looked out over the lily pond. Hanging in front of the window, spinning in the breeze, was an old-fashioned

wind-chime. With every spin the separate glass strips
struck off each other and played a magnificently random
symphony.

Evy paused for a moment to admire, then followed
her nose again out on to the screened veranda. A small
breakfast table was set up there. Two men were already
at the table, doing justice to a full breakfast. One she
knew. He looked up from his plate and smiled, that same
infectious smile she had seen the night before. He got up
from his chair and came part-way to meet her.

'Mrs Hart—what a sight you are. Good morning!'
There was something about that voice that did something to her, and she was unable to decide what it was!
Soft, reverberating, confident, trusting—oh lord,
why do I have to stop and analyse everything? she
asked herself wildly. Be natural. It's morning—a bright
tropical morning!

'What a sight I am?' she chuckled, trying to keep her
voice from giving her away. 'I thought I'd very skilfully
completed my toilette for the day. What would you have
me improve?'

'Nothing,' he said, his face turning a little red under
his magnificent tan. 'We breed big in Texas, ma'am.' He
was purposefully exaggerating his very slight drawl.
'Including big mouths. Which are very necessary, or we
would never get our foot into it, could we? That's not
what I meant. To tell the truth, ma'am, I don't see a
single thing that needs improving. Come join us for
breakfast?'

Evy smiled acceptance of his unspoken apology, and
followed him over to the table. The second man waited for
them, standing up by his chair.

'Jaime Mendoza.' Jason made the introduction with a
flourish. 'Mrs Evelyn Hart. He held her chair for her
until she was settled. 'Jaime is the manager of the *finca*,'
he explained. He used the Spanish pronunciation of the

name, 'Hy-me'. 'Another Texan, of course. Born and bred in Santurce, and educated at Texas A & M. How about that?'

'Mrs Hart,' the manager acknowledged in flawless English, with no trace of a Spanish accent. Evy took the time while Delfinia bustled in with more bacon and eggs, to examine the man. Shorter than Jason, he stood barely an inch or two above her own five foot six. His black hair lay flat, carefully combed, and matched the tiny moustache he sported. It was his arms that were impressive. Protruding from his colourful short-sleeved shirt, they showed muscles developed on top of muscles. His eyes sparkled with humour, and seemed ageless. Evy had plenty of time for her assessment, because she dared not look at Jason. That was the nub of it. She was afraid to look at Jason because it might just make her feel too good! It might turn her head, even in the daylight, as it had done in the dark of the past night!

'Something bother you?' he asked in that deep evocative voice. She shook her head and bent her face over her plate. Out of the corner of her eye she could see that he was watching her with those hawk-eyes. She tried to break away from their spell by leaning back and looking up at the ancient beams supporting the roof—and there, clinging to the beams directly over her head was a most—monstrous—thing! Unable to name it, she settled for second-best. She thrust back her chair, jumped to her feet, and started screaming.

'What is it?' Jason was at her side in a second, folding her into his protective arms before he located the danger. She was unable to answer him. Her throat was too dry, and it was hard to suppress the whimpers. All she could do was point. He followed the direction of her finger.

'Oh lord,' he sighed. 'That's Pedro. Calm down, it's only a little gecko lizard. Calm down!'

'But—but it's right inside the house,' she managed to squeeze out.

'I should hope so,' he returned, laughing. 'We spent a long time training him to stay in the house. Hey now, no more tears!' He pulled her hard up against him and turned her so she could see the little lizard clinging to the roof-stanchion.

'You trained him to stay inside?' she asked weakly. 'He looks—he looks like a Hollywood dragon. I—I'm getting your shirt wet again, aren't I?'

'I don't mind,' he said softly. 'Calmed down now?' She sniffed and wiped her eyes with the handkerchief which he had provided.

'Yes,' she stammered. 'I—I've made a fool of myself again, haven't I? What is that thing again?'

'That's Pedro. He's our house-lizard, Puerto Rican variety. He eats things, like bugs and mosquitoes and— oh, all kinds of squirmy things that we can do without. And since he's so useful, we encourage him to do his eating in the house. And when the house is extra clean, Delfinia supplements his diet. A very useful member of the family. Feel better now?'

Of course you feel better, you little fool! Evy screamed at herself. Never mind the darn lizard. Look where you are—back in his arms again. Just the thing you were going to avoid, remember? Keep your distance, be calm and cool? Remember that? Push him off now, and get about your business!

'Yes,' she said, 'I feel much better.' Her voice had a little squeak in it, and for the life of her she could not command her feet to move her away. Somehow or another her hair had come loose, falling down her back in two long braids. She nestled against the warmth of him for more seconds than required, then drove herself to step back.

'Would you prefer another breakfast plate?' asked

Jaime. 'Yours seems to have fallen on the floor.'

'No—no,' she stammered. 'I—I don't feel hungry. I—perhaps a cup of coffee?'

'And some orange juice,' Jason insisted. 'Made from our Valencia oranges. And a chunk of *pan de agua*, our Puerto Rican bread.'

Evy sipped at the glass as the two men went over their plans for the day. 'Would you like to see over the *finca*?' Jason asked her suddenly. 'You do ride, don't you?'

'Oh yes, of course I ride.' Of course. I rode in Cleveland when I was eight years old. One ride around the circle at the park, with the attendant holding the lead reins! 'Of course I ride, but I'm a little out of practice.' Which wasn't exactly a lie, was it? Besides, if it was a lie, it was worth it if I could be with him for a time. And the end justifies the means! Any fool knows that!

'Are you talking to yourself, Mrs Hart? Your lips are going a mile a minute.' And he was wearing a big grin, as if he had caught her in some terrible crime!

'I—er—I'm trying to get my lipstick on straight.'

'That's funny, I didn't think you were wearing any lipstick.'

'Yes.' It was the only answer she could bring to mind. It sounded as if it meant something, but of course it didn't. And she could see from the gleam in his eye that he knew that too.

'Jaime,' he said, 'would you get one of the men to saddle a pair of horses for us? Midnight, of course, and perhaps that little bay mare? We'll ride up through the ridge areas and check the trees.' He paused for a moment. 'And Mrs Hart, Jaime is going in to San Juan today on business. Is there anything you want from the big city?'

'No—no, thank you. I don't know anyone in the city. In fact I only stayed there for two days when I came down to the island. But I—if—it would be nice if I had my drawing board here. I need to get out two more weeks of work pretty soon.'

'That's no problem. Since you'll be here for some time, we had better have your whole kit and caboodle moved up here. But right now you had better—well, perhaps you could ride in that outfit, if you want to, but you need a hat. Get a sombrero from Delfinia, and meet me at the back steps in—oh—fifteen minutes.'

'Yes,' she said amiably, but that wasn't what she was thinking. Yes, sir! Shall I snap to it, sir? Or bow down and kiss the floor at your royal feet! Lord, what an arrogantly handsome man. Get a sombrero. Yes, sir. And strangely enough her feet carried her off to do exactly what he had ordered.

The ride turned out to be more than she had anticipated. To begin with, when they brought the horses up from the stable she was amazed to see how big they were. As best she could recall, the horses she had ridden had barely come up to the shoulder of the attendant. And here these *towered* over her. Jason swung himself up in the saddle with the ease of much practice, and then watched as she fumbled with the stirrup, wondering how in the world she was going to get her foot up that high.

'Having trouble?' he called down, and she glared up at him. All he needs to be a perfect Hollywood cowboy, she told herself grimly, is to pull out a bag of tobacco and roll his own cigarette! Damn the man! And before she could muster a witty retort he dismounted, came over to her, seized her around her tiny waist, and swung her up like a sack of beans. She grabbed desperately at the Western-style saddle horn as he measured the stirrups to her length and stuffed her feet into them.

'Next time wear a pair of shoes with heels,' he growled at her. 'And where the devil is your hat?'

'I—under the horse,' she gulped. 'It—I—it's very high up here, isn't it. What do I do with these—lines?'

'Oh lord! You said you'd ridden before!'

'I did,' she snapped back at him angrily. 'But there was a man. He held the reins and led the horse. I don't know how to steer one.'

Jason whooped with laughter, loud enough to attract the attention of several of the men who were working in the warehouse area.

'If all you have to do is make fun of me I'll pack my bag and go back to Punta Santiago,' Evy said stiffly. Her solemn pained expression cut through the laughter.

'I didn't mean to laugh *at* you,' he said quietly. 'Here's your hat. And would you be insulted if I led your horse?'

'Insulted? I thought I'd die when it looked as if I had to steer the beast myself!'

'She's not a beast. Her name is Perdita. And you needn't worry—Puerto Rican horses are bred to be sure-footed, especially in the hills. Shall we go?'

And up they *did* go, the horses walking quietly up the grassy swathe between the rows of coffee bushes, each planted carefully in the shade of taller heavily-leafed trees. 'Shade-grown coffee has a better flavour,' Jason told her as they ambled along, 'but it requires more time and more labour to bring to market. That's our big problem. We have to compete with countries that pay as little as ten cents an hour, while we have to pay the national minimum wage, which is about three dollars forty-five an hour.'

The matter under discussion was not really over Evy's head. She had the average High School education, and an interest in what he was doing. But the constant rocking as the horse ambled along was getting in the way. The saddle was highly polished, and slippery, and for some reason she could not keep her feet in the stirrups.

'Ride with your knees,' he kept telling her, but the

animal was too firmly built for her to make any impression with her knees. So when they reached the top of the ridge and pulled up she was thankful for the break. Jason lifted her down from the saddle and pointed straight ahead, over the adjacent valley.

'Our *finca* goes down the valley, and up the other side to where you see those white stone markers. That's where the Luquillo National Rain Forest begins. Those peaks over there are El Yunque, and El Toro. That's about all that's left of the tropical forest that once covered the entire island.'

Evy felt a little nervous at her surroundings. They stopped on a clear rock outcropping that overlooked the spring which was the source of the Rio Blanco. 'I—I have a fear of snakes,' she told him, trying to avoid those eyes of his.

'And about everything else in the world, I'd say. I don't know when I've met a woman with so many phobias. But you can forget about snakes on this island.'

Huh! she thought wildly. I'll bet you never had reason to be afraid of anything! It must be nice to be born heroic, with the world at your fingertips! But there was one thing about him—he was protective. If there *were* any snakes, they wouldn't *dare* to come near with him about!

'No snakes at all?' she queried. 'I thought Saint Patrick only did his thing in Ireland?'

'The name of the game around here is mongoose, not Saint Patrick. There was a time when sugar was the main crop on the island, and snakes and rats haunted the cane fields. So some enterprising Centrale owner imported several pairs of mongoose. Some came directly from India, and some from Jamaica. As a result most snakes are gone. You might occasionally see a garter snake, but the mongoose is king of the island. With no natural enemies left, they spread like wildfire.'

'Is that mongooses, or mongeese?' she asked, a tentative smile flirting at the corners of her mouth.

'Mongooses,' he laughed. 'What is this, the Inquisition? Come over here, I want to show you something.'

Evy walked to the edge of the rock. Jason put his arms around her and pointed her to a gap in the trees, through which one could see as far as the Caribbean, white-tossed in the wind. 'Straight ahead, and down.' He used one arm as a pointer and the other to hold her steady. She looked down, blankly. 'That little white area,' he coaxed. 'That's your house in the Playa de Santiago. How about that?'

How about that indeed, she sighed to herself as she leaned back against him. How about that! Both his arms were around her now, resting loosely at her waist. She lost herself in daydreams, feeling an attraction she had never known before. The smell of the thousand tiny coffee flowers, just blooming, loaded the air, and behind them two mockingbirds were battling for possession of a ramshackle nest. But all that Evy was aware of was the strength of his arms as he slowly turned her around and gently kissed her. It was not with the same driving passion as the previous night, but it was—comfortable, heartening, and no trace of panic rose to break her mood. How about that!

They returned to the house by midday, and shared a light lunch before he went into his office and closed the door behind him. Which is about all the hint a girl needs, she told herself wryly, and went back to her bedroom for a well earned siesta.

Dinner was a disappointment, for Jason had been called away. Evy heard the roar of the helicopter that swept him away, just as she was waking up from her sleep. And that seemed to put an end to the enjoyments of the day. So she dined with Maria and Delfinia, and went early to bed.

She was convinced that she had only to drop on to the massive bed to be asleep. But it didn't work out that way. She showered in the tiny attached bathroom, slipped into a lightweight nightdress, and stretched out beneath the mosquito net. Sleep would not come. Instead she daydreamed—endless pictures of Jason, rioting through her mind, doing erotic things that made her blush.

Thinking it might be the silver gleam of the moon penetrating the louvred shutters of her window that was keeping her awake, she got up again and looked out. A breeze had developed, and the long rows of trees and bushes were swaying at its command. Despite the breeze, she was still too warm. The trickle of perspiration between her breasts became a nuisance not to be borne. She shrugged her way into her light robe, put on her slippers, and went quietly out into the garden.

A procession of concrete steps led down from the high veranda to the clear area around the lily pond. Evy followed a pebbled path around to the other side of the little pool. The wind rustled her long gown. There was a feeling of—freedom—in the air. She pirouetted with both hands above her head, giggling as her skirts twirled around her. The water attracted, and she dropped to a sitting position and dipped her toes in the chilly stream.

The water was so cold she snatched her foot back—and then understood. The stream came from some of the highest mountains on the island, perhaps from the spring they had admired on their morning trip. And the water in the lily pond was not static. Static water bred mosquitoes, mosquitoes bred malaria, malaria bred death. Evy smiled at her naïve ability to draw conclusions, pulling her knees up to her chin and folding her arms around her lower limbs. Reason resolves everything, her prim little conscience told her. She laughed at herself, and stood up.

The moon, and the beautiful white blossoms of the *campagna de noche* took her interest—so much so that she failed to hear the padding of feet behind her, and when the massively-haired male arm came around from behind and clamped a hand over her mouth she was momentarily paralysed.

But only momentarily. She was a coward, and would be the first to admit it to anyone. She had a coward's over-abundance of 'fight or flight' adrenalin. The hand that tried to seal her mouth slipped slightly, just enough for her to get her mouth open and her teeth apart. With all the strength that fear provided she clamped down on the soft flesh under his thumb and drove her sharp little teeth in as deeply as she could. His hand dropped away.

There was no need for her to scream. He did it for her. He danced around in circles making loud animal noises, holding one bleeding hand up over his head with the other. The noise awoke the house. Evy could see the lights snap on, and, silhouetted against them, another man coming towards her out of the darkness. He had both hands extended to grab her. She ducked under them, plucked up her skirt as high as she could, and raced back the way she had come, towards the house.

The second man saw her movement, and by a change of direction managed to get in front of her again. Without thinking she turned uphill, losing her slippers as she struggled out of the house-clearing and into the cluster of lemon and orange trees that filled a small triangle just above the house.

Behind her she could hear the uproar from the garden, where her first assailant was still bellowing in pain. She could also hear the footsteps and the panting breath behind her, as if her pursuer was not in too good a condition. But he was still coming.

She looked around for some open avenue, but found

none. The moon was setting, distorting the light. Her movements were almost mindless, controlled by that deep stratum of mind that had served the caveman. Rather than run farther in the darkness, she stopped, selected a large tree, and huddled herself down against its bole on the side away from the footsteps. She froze herself into position, head down; somewhere she had once read that it was the brightness of a face that gave fugitives away. The footsteps came up to her position, hesitated, then continued on up the hill. Evy held her breath, not sure what to do next. And as she thought, the moon dropped behind the western mountains and the area became completely black.

The noises from the house, below her, died out. The screaming man had either been silenced, or—was coming up the hill after her? And the one who had passed her had not returned. Not yet! She could hear a voice from below her, in the house, so clear that she could almost be standing at the elbow of the speaker. It was Maria's voice, high-pitched with anxiety.

'I have look in her room, *señor*. My *mariposa no es aqui!* She have gone!'

Stand up and go back, Evy told herself firmly. The command unlocked her tortured arms and legs, and she struggled to her feet. Her legs were trembling, hardly able to bear her weight. And there was another padding of feet below her. Someone was coming up the side of the mountain!

Her mind surrendered control of her body, and panic seized her. She fled sideways, along the rim of the hill, bashing her way through the tiny underbrush that clung in clumps between the lemon trees. Her gown and hair streamed behind her in the breeze as she ran, creating the look of a ghost fleeing through the fragrant grove. By luck more than by reason she avoided running into trees, but sharp rocks penetrated the skin of her bare feet, and only fear kept her going. Run, her mind screamed at her, run!

Through the lemon grove, out on to the dirt road that led up the mountain, and into the safety of the dark coffee plantation she ran. It was easier here. The coffee bushes were planted farther apart than the lemon trees, and the ground around them was matted with soft undergrowth. But because the coffee was grown in the shade of the larger trees there was less light than before.

She was losing her breath. The adrenalin had pumped up her muscles for a time, but that time was passed. When she suddenly ran full-face into an obstacle, she had no more strength, and no more courage to run. She slumped down, leaning against the obstacle, slowly slipping to the ground. But a pair of arms came around her, and she could feel that indefinable comfort that told her who it was.

'Whoa now,' he said quietly, cuddling her head against his chest. 'Whoa now—everything is okay. We got him. You're safe.'

Mentally and physically exhausted, Evy accepted his strength and assurance. And now that she was safe, womanlike, she began to cry. Tears dripped down her cheeks and on to his bare chest. As she brushed against him her senses told her that he was wearing only a pair of ragged shorts. It made him seem more real, more comforting. She slipped her arms around his waist and pressed her breasts against him, squirming to get closer to the safety he represented. He held her gently until the tears stopped.

'There now. All cried out?'

'There was a second man,' she stammered. 'He chased me up the mountain. He—'

'It's all right,' he repeated. 'I've got six of the toughest mountain men you ever saw—real *jibaros*. They're searching the area with our dogs. If he's still here we'll get him. Okay?'

'Okay,' she murmured, and drew herself up against him again. A moment of silence passed. 'I'm such a coward,' she whispered to him. In the shroud of darkness she would make no attempt to sustain her pride. 'He jumped me from behind. I had to come all the way to Puerto Rico to get mugged! God, once I thought I was as tough a girl as any foster-programme could produce, yet now everything scares me. What do they want from me?'

'I don't know. But we'll find out. And you'd better stay with me until we solve the puzzle. There must be an easy answer, but I don't know what it is—yet! And I promise you that nothing like this will ever happen to you again. Believe me?' One of his fingers tipped her chin up, but it was so dark under the trees that she could not see his face.

Her hands wandered up and caressed his face. 'Yes,' she whispered, 'I believe you.' I'll believe *anything* at this moment, she told herself. Anything! Just so long as he holds me, he keeps me safe from the whole world. If only I could live like this for ever, locked safely in his arms!

'Let's start back towards the house,' Jason prompted her. She half turned, so that her body was parallel to his, and with his arms still tight around her shoulders. She took a trembling step forward, more a shuffle than a step, perhaps, for her foot caught in a ground vine that tripped her. He clutched at her, but she pulled him off balance, and they both landed on the soft turf of the well-carpeted plantation. One of his hands ventured down her leg, looking for damage. It found the leakage of blood that oozed from the scratches and cuts the bottom of her feet had accumulated during her flight.

'Great day,' he grunted. 'No wonder you can't walk, Mrs Hart.' He scrambled back to his feet, then swung her up in his arms. 'And I can't go on calling you Mrs Hart. Not after this wild day.'

'No—no, of course not,' she gasped shyly. 'My—my name is Evelyn. My acquaintances call me Eve. My friends call me Evy.'

'And am I a friend of yours—Evy?'

She was close enough now to see the smile on his face, the glitter in his eyes, and the lock of raven hair that had fallen down on his forehead. She used one finger to brush it back, then she put both arms around his neck and kissed him gently.

'Is that a friendly kiss?' he probed.

She studied him as best she could, not sure how much she ought to admit. 'Not exactly,' she whispered, 'but you could call me Evy anyway.'

'Ah!' He chuckled, turned around with her weight in his arms, and started to walk through the trees. They were strong arms, supporting her heart and spirit as well as her body. She relaxed against him, enjoying the interplay of his shoulder muscles as they shifted back and forth. He stopped for a moment to catch his bearings. As he looked around, her fingers gently stroked the side of his face, where her nails had done so much damage the day before, and he laughingly snapped his teeth in the direction of her fingers. She pulled her hand away, knowing that he was not really angry, and he started off again.

'How can you possibly know where we are?' she asked tentatively a few minutes later. Jason stopped again, bent his head, and kissed the tip of her nose. 'Doubting Thomasina?' he asked. 'I know the layout of this *finca* like the palm of my hand, lady.'

'Well, if that's so,' she laughed up at him, 'how come we don't see the lights of the house from here?'

'Because, first of all, the house is entirely buried by the trees that surround it,' he snorted, 'and secondly, the electric power has gone off again—as usual. Don't you know nothing? Were you never a Boy Scout?'

'I don't think so,' she answered primly. 'And if you know all that much, where the devil are we?'

'For your information,' he returned, 'we're very close to the swimming pool. There's a path there that leads directly back to the house.'

'Am I getting too heavy for you?'

'I wish you hadn't said that,' he sighed, letting her feet drop to the ground. 'In the movies the hero can carry his lady for miles and miles. Stand still while I get my breath back, then we'll be on our way.'

'I could walk—well, at least I could hobble—some,' she suggested.

'You've beaten down my male ego enough already,' he told her, and swung her back up in his arms. 'Now you just nestle back there quietly and I'll have you back to the house in a jiffy. We're only a step or two from the swimming pool now.'

They were both laughing when he took that step. All she knew of it was a muttered noise he made that sounded almost like 'Oh hell!' before she slipped forward in the darkness, still in his arms, and they both fell into the deep end of the pool.

It was the shocking coldness of the water that inspired her to move. She came to the surface like a long-distance swimmer, her long nightgown trailing behind her like the sea-queen's cloak. As his head surfaced beside her she turned over on her stomach and began a racing crawl for the end of the pool. Jason caught up with her as she reached the steps, and loaned her a hand as she struggled to get her legs untangled from the gown.

They sat on the edge of the pool, dripping cold mountain spring water off in all cascading directions. Evy flipped her hair forward over her arm and wrung it out. Her teeth were chattering. 'It will be a medical first,' she told him solemnly. 'I shall be the first person ever to freeze to death on a tropical island.'

'But I was right, wasn't I?' He was trying to laugh through his own quaking teeth. 'Admit it, I was right!'

'Right about what?'

'I said we were only a step or two from the swimming pool, didn't I?'

'Wise guy,' she muttered, squeezing up against him. Even soaking wet he was a comfort. His arms came around her, drawing her closer. She stretched up so she could nuzzle his cheek. His hands moved down to her waist, where the thinness of her wet gown left nothing to the imagination, and he stroked her shivering form from waist down to the full curve of her hips.

'Hadn't we better use that path to the house before we both catch pneumonia?' she prodded, not sure she could stand too much of the sensation his moving hands were causing.

'Spoilsport,' he answered. 'What's the big hurry? We'll dry out in a few minutes.'

'Sure we will, and be frozen solid when we do.'

'Don't interrupt, woman. Who knows what we might find to do by way of entertainment? Is there something important that you need to do up at the house?'

And there's the challenge, Evy told herself, a little downhearted. You knew it had to come some time—but why so soon? Just a few days more—maybe even one day—and I might have built up my courage enough to—to do it. But here it is. Here and now. Come into my parlour, said the spider!

'Yes,' she sighed. I need to think. I need to evaluate what's going on. I need to regain control of this panicky world of mine, so I can see clearly what I should do.

'Yes,' she repeated, 'I need to cut my fingernails!'

CHAPTER FOUR

THE long night was too much for Evy. By the time they had found the path to the house, dried themselves off, and drunk a hot rum toddy, it was three o'clock in the morning. She tumbled into bed, exhausted, and did not stir again until the birds squabbling outside the window forced her to open an eye. At the same moment Maria came in with a breakfast tray.

Evy stretched slowly, moving every muscle at her command, but slowly. 'I seem to be all bruises,' she complained to the older woman. 'Every bone aches—and even my aches have aches!'

'You have a hard day yesterday,' Maria responded as she bustled about, setting up the breakfast tray by the window. 'Oh, those crazy birds! They make so much noise, no?'

'I don't mind them.' She struggled out of bed and blearily searched for her robe. 'Pigeons are friendly creatures.'

Maria poked her head out the window for a closer look. 'What you think,' she laughed. 'Not pigeons—mocking birds. Delfinia says they are all over the farm. They eat the coffee fruit, fight in the trees, imitate everything they hear. Crazy!'

Evy lowered herself gingerly into the chair by the window, wincing as she walked. The bottoms of her feet were still tender, but otherwise all right. 'I can understand why I'm so bruised around the shoulders,' she complained, 'but why do I have this funny feeling about sitting down?'

'Is the horses,' said Maria very practically. 'Puerto

Rican horses are bred to walk safely on the mountains, no? But inside they are stuffed with iron, not hay! At least, I think so. I must ask Ramón. Now, what you want to wear this afternoon?'

'This afternoon? Let me get through the morning first!'

'You already finish with the morning,' Maria told her. 'Is now the afternoon already. Crazy mainlanders, no? You stay in bed until siesta, then you want to get up!' The words by themselves might have been a complaint, but spoken with a broad loving smile, there was no sting to them.

'You could be my mother,' Evy commented impulsively.

'*Madre de Dios*—no! *Abuela, si.* Mother? Never happens! I am too old for your generation, *linda*. So you eat up now. *El Jefe* says to me and Delfinia—we should be enough to fatten you up! He wants you should be—more of you—you understand?'

'Well, you can tell him that there's plenty of me now for my own satisfaction,' Evy snapped at her. 'Where is he now?'

'He works in the office. And you can tell him for yourself, no? Always when a man worries about a woman who does not eat, that is not something for others to interfere in, *comprendo*? He likes his women to be more—comfortable for hugging, no?'

'How do I know, Maria? I'm not one of his women!' Evy did her best to look disdainful and uninterested, but was unable to hold the pose. When she broke out in giggles Maria shook her head sadly. No doubt about it, these Norteamericanas had forgotten some very important things in their drive to equality and independence. Like, how to please a man. She sniffed audibly.

'Oh, I have forget to tell you,' Maria recollected. 'There is someone who waits to see you—my grandson

Ramón. You remember him? Why he does not get along better in the Policia I do not know. Such a smart boy. I remember, for his confirmation, the—ah, but I forget. Is not my grandson who waits, it is a policeman. Don't dress too fancy—not for a policeman!'

'But I could dress fancy for your grandson?' Evy got up from the table having consumed everything in sight. 'That was wonderfully fresh French bread. I really love that!'

Maria was all smiles as she took out of the clothes closet a simple white shirtwaister dress, and laid it out over a chair. 'You talk like the tourists, *linda*. Because bread is baked a certain way it must be French bread? Nonsense! That is old-fashioned Spanish bread you have eat. We call it *pan de agua*. Delfinia bakes three times a week. How about this dress, huh? Is halfway.'

Evy raised her eyebrows. 'Halfway?'

'Halfway between dress-up for my grandson, and pay-no-attention for the policeman, no?'

Rather than make Ramón wait, Evy brushed her hair lightly, then left it loose, fashioned in ponytail. Ramón was sitting out on the veranda. Jason was with him.

Evy stopped in the doorway to assess them. Another habit of her youth. In one word, sum up the person you are about to meet. For Ramón, comforting. For Jason? Passionate? Magnetic? Or that other word that she refused to consider. One could hardly apply a word like 'loving' to someone who is practically a stranger! She smoothed down her dress, patted her hair, and went out to meet them both.

'*Señora!*' The detective rose to his feet and bowed slightly from the waist. Jason, who was already standing, winked at her and then imitated the bow. He guided her to a chair. As she sat, Ramón dropped gratefully on to the divan.

'It has been a long night,' the detective sighed. 'And you are well?'

'Very well,' she said. Jason was standing just behind her chair. She raised her arm in his direction, and his hand touched her arm just at the elbow and squeezed it gently.

'So.' Ramón fumbled through his notebook, and found a stub of a pencil in his shirt pocket. 'This man in the garden last night—his name is Fuentes. One of those Cubans, you understand.' His nose wrinkled, as if the word tasted badly. 'He is what you would call in New York a punk—a minor gangster. He is faced with assault charges, and attempted kidnapping, which oils the tongue, you understand. The other man, he thinks he has gotten away from us. He is up in the hills. A city man—we will have him soon. Do you know this man Fuentes?'

'Know him? Of course not,' she said. 'How would I know a man like that?'

'That brings up an interesting question, Mrs Hart. I have talked to the *policia* in Cleveland, and they have no record there of a Mrs Evelyn Hart. What do you make of that?'

For a moment she was dumbfounded. What do you make of that? She had not really thought about the subject when she had given him her name. Of course there was no record of a Mrs Evelyn Hart. But what had that to do with this Cuban? Think carefully, she told herself. Policemen make very poor confidantes. Very poor. Everything you say may be taken down and used against you in court!

'I—I don't know what to say,' she quavered. The hand holding hers squeezed gently.

'What you should say,' Ramón went on, 'is your real name, Mrs Santuccio. That is your real name, isn't it?'

There seemed to be no use trying to hide something he already knew. 'Yes, Mrs Evelyn Hart Santuccio.'

The detective snapped his book shut and tapped its cover a couple of times. 'Your husband, Mrs Santuccio, was a soldier in the Cleveland Syndicate. You were aware of that?'

'Please—don't call me that,' she said raggedly. 'I haven't used that name in two years or more.' She sat up straight in her chair, holding her muscles rigid to stop the tremors. 'It's not illegal for a widow to use her maiden name!'

'No, of course not. Except if it is done to defraud someone,' he said softly. 'But you did know about your husband?'

'Yes, I knew,' she sighed. 'Towards the end I knew. But he never amounted to much. You called him a soldier—he was really only a messenger—a runner. He talked big, but he wasn't.'

'We're just looking for a link, Mrs Hart. Your husband was a member of the Cleveland crime family. Your house is under surveillance by local members of the Cuban connection. And somebody tried to kidnap you. It all adds up.'

'To what?' interjected Jason. 'Are you suggesting that Evy had something to do with the mob?'

'If I knew what it added up to the case would be solved,' said Ramón as he got up and slid his notebook back in his pocket. 'But in any case, *amigo*, you will see that Mrs Hart is protected? At all times, you understand?'

'Of course I will,' Jason snapped. 'Jaime is moving into the house, and a couple of the *jibaros* who live off the farm are coming in to stay—for as long as necessary.'

'Don't be too sure of yourself,' Ramón told him. 'They will know about that in San Juan before nightfall. Nothing is secret on this island—you know that. You have taken steps against what they did last night. Give some thought to what comes next. If you keep your eye on yesterday, who will be watching for what comes tonight? *Adios, señora*—Jason.'

The detective disappeared, and so did Jason. 'I have a big problem involving some investments in Grenada,' he told her as he went out. 'Why don't you take a lazy afternoon at the swimming pool?' They had stopped at the half-opened door of the office. Inside Evy could see banks of radios, teletype machines, and two large television sets. He followed her eyes.

'It's a communications centre,' he explained. 'I have contact by satellite and by cable with every one of the Caribbean offices of the family, and a direct connection with our fairly large computer in San Juan. The computer lives in the city so that I can live in the country. How's that?'

She smiled up at him, bemused by his expression, confused by the banks of equipment with which he seemed so conversant. 'It's all Greek to me,' she sighed. 'I should go to the pool?'

'Of course.' He patted her hand and ushered her towards the door. 'It's heated by solar panels during the daytime. At night it's water just off the glacier.'

'There isn't any glacier in the tropics,' she teased. 'Do you think I'm really that stupid?'

'If I were to tell you what I thought you were, it would take more than a week or two. Now, go squeeze into a bathing suit and get gone, Evy Hart.' He pushed her gently out the door and closed it behind her.

And so much for you, Evy Hart, she told herself derisively. If it's true that he wants you as entertainment, it's only part-time entertainment! Never let a little romance interfere between me and my business, huh? Look at the difference between us, girl. He's locked up in his room talking to the world, and you're standing outside in the hall talking to yourself! Doesn't that tell you? What I need is a big 'keep off' sign that I can hang around his neck just to remind me!

The pool did a little something towards calming her mind. The solar panels were very effective. The water in the pool was at air temperature, seventy-five degrees. She swam back and forth for a few exercise laps, finding that her muscles were gradually relaxing. Then she climbed out and moved over to one of the lounge chairs, stretched out in the shade of her sun hat and dark glasses, and promptly fell asleep.

It was about an hour later that she woke up, triggered by the shade that was obscuring her from the sun. She pushed her big hat back and squinted with one eye. Standing next to her chair was a well-dressed woman. Evy managed to assemble herself and stood up. 'I'm Evelyn Hart,' she said, holding out a hand. It was ignored. The woman was a typical Spanish beauty, taller than Evy, with pale white skin and dark hair, deep brown eyes, dressed in a clinging black dress, with absurdly high-heeled shoes. Her fingers were loaded with rings. All except the third finger of her left hand.

'So—you are the little blonde that Jason is playing with this week,' she said. Her voice was deep, soft, and mellow.

'Well, I—I wouldn't say that,' Evy returned weakly. Despite all her experience, she had a major weakness. When boldly attacked she hardly knew what to do. By tomorrow, she knew, she would think of a most merciless comeback to that statement—but for today, there was no witticism she could muster.

'I would,' the brunette said sharply. 'I am Francisca de Molinaro. You have heard of me?'

'I—I'm new to the area,' Evy equivocated. 'I—no, I haven't.'

'Too bad. You should have. That was naughty of Jason. Among other things, I am Jason's fiancée. You understand that word, I suppose?'

'Jason's—you and Jason are—you plan to marry?'

'Ah! It surprises you? Yes, Jason and I are going to marry, very soon. But then it should not bother you. You are already married, I understand. It is Mrs Hart, isn't it?'

'Yes, it's Mrs Hart,' Evy returned coldly. So what? It could only be a week-end affair, anyway. It isn't as if I were deeply in love with him and wanted to spend the rest of my life with him, is it? Jason is yours, and you've come to reclaim him, like a lost parcel, or something. If he were mine, believe me, I'd never leave him lying around for some dumb blonde to pick up. And of course that was the weakest spot in this woman's story! Jason just wasn't the man you left lying around. And she wore no engagement ring! Jason wasn't the sort of man who left his filly around unbranded, was he? So why should I just take her word for all this, because—because he *is* just the man I would want to spend the rest of my life with, that's why!

And having finally made that admission to herself, Evy Hart was prepared to play whatever game this young lady wanted to play. Young lady? She looked to be almost Jason's age—thirty, or thirty-five perhaps? Only a splendid make-up job was hiding the little cracks around her mouth, and the slackness of her jaw! Meeoow, Evy told herself. Pay attention!

'Won't you sit down?' she invited. 'I'll call Delphinia to bring us something cool to drink.'

'Don't bother. I know this house as if it were my own. I've already told the housekeeper what my requirements are.'

'How nice,' Evy responded, completely at a loss for something else to say. Francisca smiled bleakly at her, and folded herself down gracefully on the adjacent lounge chair.

'Now then, Mrs—er—Hart,' she said, 'tell me all about yourself.' It was a command that Evy was not about to honour. The less anyone knew about her, the happier she would be. Information is like a weapon, like a sharp unsheathed sword. She offered the other woman a plastic smile as Maria came out with a tray and glasses.

'For the lady, a Cuba Libre,' announced Maria. 'For you, *mariposa*, the orange juice, no? And be careful. Not too much sun!' The old lady smiled at them and walked away.

'You make friends with the servants?'

'Maria is not a servant. She is my *dueña*. What does that mean, *mariposa*?'

'It is a name given to very small children. It means little butterfly—a child's name. And a married woman doesn't require a *dueña*. Especially not an old busybody like that one. Are you related to her?'

'Yes,' Evy returned, and laughed inwardly at the shock in the other woman's face, 'we are closely related. She is my grandmother.'

The other woman smiled again, a cold calculating smile. 'It is better to say nothing than to lie,' she said, sipping at her tall cold glass. 'I know about you, Mrs Hart. And what a lie that name is! You were born and brought up in Cleveland, Ohio, so that woman could hardly be your grandmother. And you were married there too! Poor man. What did you do to him that made him take his own life?'

'What—what do you mean?' stammered Evy. 'Take his own life? My husband died in an accident. And how do you know anything about Frank?'

'Oh, we know a great deal about you, Mrs Hart. A very great deal. So just how did you drive Frank to take his own life?'

'God, what a monster you are!' Evy snapped. 'Even if it were true—which it isn't—you have no right to talk to me like that!'

'No right?' Francisca's lovely voice tinkled like a bell. 'You've imposed yourself on my fiancé's house and time, with some crazy trumpled-up story about needing protection. From what? Just what are you doing here, Mrs Santuccio?'

Evy blanched and lost control of herself. She struggled up from the lounge chair, hurt showing plainly on her gentle face, and ran for the house, tears blurring her eyes. What did I do to him that made him take his own life? she asked herself. What? She didn't need Francisca de Molinaro to haunt her. She had asked herself the question countless times before. She clattered down the hall, slammed her way into the safety of her own bedroom, and threw herself down on the bed, crying. Which was the condition that Maria found her in at seven o'clock, when she came in to remind her to dress for dinner.

With the help of considerable make-up and some specialised advice from Maria, Evy managed to recover her aplomb. There was a small group in the living room having a pre-dinner drink. Jaime stood by the door with a rum colada in his hand. Jason stood by the fireplace. Francisca was beside him, holding a small glass in one hand, and using the other to stroke Jason's forearm. Francisca was wearing an off-the-shoulder white sheath that clung to her like a second skin. Around her neck hung a gleaming course of deep-set emeralds, and her hair gleamed raven-black against the white orchid tucked behind her ear. Evy looked down at her own three-quarter-length blue nothing, and sighed. Outmanoeuvred again! When the dress had once fitted her, three years ago, she had bulged in all the right places, and it made a very satisfactory statement about her.

Now she was twenty pounds lighter, all it said was 'disaster'! And there was no way her imitation pearls could outwrestle those beautiful emeralds. For one jealous moment Evy was tempted to steal back down the corridor, and hide in her bedroom again. But there was no easy escape.

'Evy!' called Jason, and she walked over to him. 'I want you to meet an old family friend. This is Francisca de Molinaro. Francisca, Evelyn Hart.'

'Miss Molinaro and I have already met,' Evy said softly. 'We were at the pool together earlier. An old family friend?'

Jason displayed that grin again. 'Yes. Accent on friend, not on old. Our families lived side by side when we were all young. Francisca went to school with my sister. And Fran is going to honour us by staying over for a few days. Won't that be grand? She's an old Puerto Rican hand, she can probably give you some pointers while I'm working.'

The two women exchanged dagger thrusts under his nose, but he failed to notice. I'll bet she wants to give me some pointers! Evy told herself. All on daggers—or arrows—straight through the heart. How about that for a local joke? She wants to shoot me right through the Hart! It was so bad that even Evy couldn't bring herself to laugh.

Jaime came over to join them. He nodded briefly at Evy, but his interest seemed to lie entirely with Francisca. 'There's a fiesta tomorrow night at Ponce,' he said. 'We could all go to that. I'm sure Mrs Hart would enjoy it.'

Francisca looked at him strangely, then smiled. 'A fine idea,' she agreed. 'I'd forgotten how much fun those little fiestas can be. Will there be costumes and dancing?'

'Whether there will be or not doesn't count,' Jason interrupted gruffly. 'Mrs Hart will not be leaving the bounds of the *finca*, at least not for some time. Shall we go in to dinner?'

He offered his arm to Francisca, who was closest to him. She took it with an arch smile, and the two of them started out to the veranda. Jaime looked at Evy with disappointment in his eyes, but offered her an arm. She took it. Two losers, walking together, she told herself as they came to the table.

Dinner was more elaborate than on her first night, but still entirely in the island mode. *Gandule* soup was served, followed by *lechon asado*, the highly spiced roast pig, still cooked over a charcoal fire, as in the old days. Along with the *lechon*, backed *chayotes*, the tropical equivalent of a squash, was served. The salad was *palmillo*, from the heart of the palm tree. And the inevitable side-dish of *arroz con habituellos* that seemed to make it to the table in every Puerto Rican home—rice and beans!

The conversation did not match the food. Francisca managed to keep her subjects among the 'you remember when' area, cutting Evy out entirely. Jaime, after trying to share with Jason, finally gave up, and spent the evening educating Evy on the subject of coffee growing, and why it was nothing like the television ads on Columbian coffee. She did her best to keep up her side, but it was hard, almost impossible, in fact. How do you smile as someone describes the long involved process of freeing the coffee bean from the ripe coffee cherry fruit, when your heart and soul are engaged in trying to overhear what is going on at the other side of the table? And what made it worse was that Jason seemed to be eating it all up. His eyes were glued to the lovely Spanish face, following her stories with laughter, allowing her hand to rest on his arm interminably.

But at least I'm not alone, Evy told herself. Every time Francisca's hand touched Jason's arm, Jaime jumped and a pained expression flashed across his face. Only when the places were cleared and they were concentrating on the desert, an ice-cream mixed with perfect slices of the native Valencia oranges, did the older woman turn to the other two at the table.

'You must excuse me,' she said condescendingly, 'but it's been a very long time since Jason and I have had a chance to talk together. I am so busy in San Juan, you know. It's almost like a madhouse down there. But then you know a great deal about madhouses, don't you, Mrs Hart?'

Her words struck Evy like a bolt of lightning. You know a great deal about madhouses, Mrs Hart. What should I say? Oh yes, some of my best friends are mad? Or, I've seen more common sense and compassion inside the sanitarium than outside? How in God's name could she know about that? Not for anything would I ever had told anyone. How does she know? Does she know? It took only a quick look at that chiselled face to be sure that Francisca de Molinaro knew—not guessed. She knew! Faced with the hard facts, Evy decided to attack.

'I must bow to your expertise,' she said softly. 'With so much crime and passion on the streets it's hard to tell whether or not *we* ought to be confined, and the inmates let go. Don't you think so?'

'Perhaps it seems that way only in Ohio,' Francisca returned. 'That is your home state, is it not?'

'It is, yes, but how did you know?' interrupted Jason, and Francisca's claws instantly disappeared.

'Oh, I really don't know. Somebody told me, or I read it in the papers or something like that. Or perhaps I read it in one of her cartoons. I'm an avid reader of your strip, Mrs Hart.'

'I'll bet you must be,' Evy said sarcastically. 'It's drawn for children, but of course we have many adult readers. Were you disappointed when I killed off Alfred the Elephant?'

'Oh yes, terribly so. Such a sweet character. But I suppose you just had to do it?'

'Yes, of course,' Evy returned. Yes, of course, you fake. There never was an elephant in my strip, and never will be. Just what is your game, Miss Molinaro? Her train of thought was interrupted, as both Maria and Delfinia came in to clear away the table.

'We'll have coffee inside,' said Jason. They all rose to go into the living room, when Delfinia came back into the room with a worried look on her face. 'There is a radio call, *señor*,' she said. 'Something about an accident at the petro-chemical plant.'

'I'll come at once,' said Jason. 'You'd better come too, Jaime. We'll leave the ladies to their coffee and gossip.'

Won't that be grand! Evy chided herself as she followed Francisca unwillingly out on to the veranda. The older woman took pride of place on the divan, while Evy made do with a hard-backed single chair. Why make myself comfortable? she asked herself. I'm not going to enjoy this, so I might as well be thoroughly miserable!

Delfinia came in with the coffee tray. From the look on her face she appreciated Francisca as little as Evy did. She plopped the tray down on the coffee table between them and left as if the devil himself were after her.

Francisca poured as if she were the mistress of the house. Evy accepted a cup, stirred it gently, and sipped. They were so quiet that other sounds supervened. The cicadas were hard at work in the bushes below them. A hunting owl hooted high up on the mountain, and the *coqui*, the tree frog whose sound gave it its name, backed them all up with a chorus.

'So, you have given any more thought to our earlier conversation?' Francisca put her cup down on the table and bent forward to watch Evy closely.

'I can't say that I have,' Evy returned. 'What part exactly are you interested in discussing? Your engagement to Jason?'

'There is nothing to discuss there,' the older woman replied. 'It's a fact. We merely await the time – the proper time, mind you.'

'Something is holding up your wedding plans? From your conversation at the table you haven't seen much of Jason lately, have you?'

'We don't live in each other's pockets, if that's what you mean. We have a firm understanding. Jason is a very busy man, as you can see. And I—I lead a very busy life, also.'

'Oh? What exactly is it that you do?'

'How ignorant you are, my dear. I operate a fashion house in the capital city. In San Juan.'

'Fashions? How nice for you. Do you design what you sell?'

'Well, really, you can't expect a Molinaro to mingle with tradesmen, can you? Yes, I design the clothing. There are boutiques that sell for me. Although I do occasionally model my own creations from time to time, you understand, just to keep in touch with the customers.'

And what do you say to that, Evy Hart? Once again Evy felt tongue-tied, unable to find an answer. 'How nice for you,' she managed to grind out.

'Indeed,' returned Francisca, sounding very satisfied with herself. 'And of course when Jason and I are married I shall do much better—because of the backing of his family, you understand. We are all very close, and as you heard, Lucy and I went to school together. At the convent school, of course.'

'Of course.' What else does one say? Too bad you didn't choke to death? Just exactly how rarefied *is* the air you breathe? Damn! Damn! Damn! If only I could find some chink in her armour. And then it came to her.

'You know what makes it all seem to be a fairy tale,' she asked innocently. 'You don't seem to have an engagement ring!'

'Oh, that. You poor innocent child! I can see it all now. You think that just because Jason has wined you and kissed you and taken you to his bed, he's madly in love with you? You blush? But it's all true, isn't it, you little fool! There is no possible way that a person of your background could possibly fit into the life that Jason and I, and his family, lead. No possible way. Surely you can see not only what pain this continued pretence would bring you, but what difficulty you make for Jason when he has to cast you off? Why don't you just give it up, Mrs Hart? Jason is mine, and I intend to stay here long enough to discourage little poachers like you from trying to steal him from me. Why don't you just go home?'

'That's a great deal of talk, Miss Molinaro,' Evy maintained stoutly, 'but you still don't wear his engagement ring!'

'My poor dear child,' Francisca sighed. 'You just never will fit in, will you? Let me explain. We Puerto Ricans live in a double culture. We follow the American and the Spanish. And in the Spanish tradition an engagement is announced by the giving of a bracelet, not a ring. A bracelet like this one.'

Her hand slipped casually to her right wrist, and she rotated a plain gold bracelet, inset with diamonds, so that the light glistened off their facets. Evy stared at it, mesmerised, while the Spanish woman continued to rotate the bracelet back and forth, gleefully. Could it be true? Did the Spanish tradition require a bracelet? And if so, would Jason follow the Spanish rather than the American tradition? Her hands shivered as they tightened on the arms of the chair. Of course it could be so.

Could be, and probably was. For the second time in one day, Evy turned tail. With a choking sob she sprang to her feet and dashed down the hall, almost knocking Jason over in her flight from torment. And as she fled she could hear the high-pitched laughter behind her, as Francisca celebrated her victory.

It rang in Evy's ears long after she had slammed the bedroom door behind her.

CHAPTER FIVE

SHE awoke early to a room full of sunshine, and the same quarrelsome birds chattering away in the branch of the *ceiba* tree, just outside her window. For the first time since she had come to El Semillo she had the time and the desire to look around her bedroom. My crying room, she told herself, and had the humour to laugh wryly at herself. It was not a huge room, as such rooms go in old houses, but it was about fifteen feet wide and perhaps twenty-five feet long. The walls were panelled, in some wood that gleamed darkly in the morning light, as if years of polishing had been the order of many days. The floor too was of the same dark wood, but tessellated. A huge white rug took pride of place beside the bed. The bed itself was a four-poster, with an intricately carved headboard, and the ever-present canopy for the mosquito net. A large bureau, two clothes closets, and four scattered chairs made up the budget of furniture. Through a tiny slit in the bottom of the closet doors Evy could see the light that burned permanently within, to provide the heat that fought tropical mildew.

She bounced out of bed, full of energy, and in surprisingly good spirits. If all this weeping does anything, she thought, at least it's provided early nights and more rest than usual! She strolled over to the mirror that hung on the wall above the bureau, and for the first time in years she examined Evelyn Hart.

The girl was almost a stranger to her. Her gaunt face, slimmed almost to the bones, had a look of haunting weariness about it. The dimples were still present, but now had become tiny dots in her tightly stretched skin.

76

There was a permanent frown lurking on the edges of her mouth, but the widespread eyes and cool forehead reflected a balance of beauty she had never recognised before. Almost unbelieving she ran the palm of her hand up over one cheek. 'Pinch me and see if I'm real,' she murmured to herself, and did so. 'Damn!' she muttered. 'Don't be so enthusiastic!'

A clatter of utensils cracked on her ear. I must be right over the kitchen, she thought. And with that little prompting her stomach sent up 'empty' messages to her brain. Better hurry, she told herself. She saluted her mirror image with a thrown kiss and dived into the bathroom.

Designed for women, she told herself—small, but everything ultra-modern, in a pattern of gold and pink that soothed the eye. One whole wall was mirrored. She slipped out of her utilitarian granny nightgown, and set the shower temperature to her taste. The mirrored wall reflected her faithfully. Her full firm figure was gone. She could count her ribs, projecting through almost translucent skin. Her tiny waist had shrunk, and although her hips swelled outward gracefully, there were bony projections where once soft flesh had curved.

Only her breasts remained the same, high, firm, full. And looking even more so because of the skimpiness of the rest of her. That, and my hair, she sighed, that's all I have to offer now. She flipped the swathe of thick blonde hair that hung loosely past her shoulders. I must get it cut some day, she thought as she stepped into the shower stall. Evy Hart, on display. Luckily I'm no longer man-hunting! I would have to find one who didn't mind chancing splinters when he hugged me! But for all that, a fine figure of a woman, even though it's all second-hand goods!

She was still thinking in that vein, and laughing, as she

struggled to brush the mass of her still-wet hair. And at that point Maria knocked and came in.

'*Buenos dias, linda*. It is a fine day again. The rainy season is over, and the spring have come, no?'

'I suppose so.' Evy followed Maria back out to the bedroom, struggling with her hair while the older woman pulled back the curtains. 'It's hard getting accustomed to spring beginning in February!'

'Ah, you will learn. But I forget something. *El Jefe* say to invited you to breakfast and go riding with him, please? He say especially I should say please.'

'*El Jefe?* Who in the world is that?'

'You must learn Spanish, *linda*. Everybody on this island speak English and Spanish, except you, no? *El Jefe* means the boss—Don Jason. What I tell him?'

Evy's mind danced. *El Jefe* says please. To the devil with Francisca Molinaro! 'Tell him yes, thank you.' She put away the dress she had been contemplating and pulled out a pair of jeans for practicality, and a thin white tie-neck blouse for show. And don't forget the sombrero, she reminded herself as she walked happily out on to the veranda.

Jason was alone at the breakfast table, looking much as she remembered him on their first day. But today he was dressed casually in jeans, open-neck shirt, and boots. He held her chair, then joined her. 'Something substantial this morning? Eggs, ham, *pan de agua*, *habituelles*? Coffee?'

'Oh, I love that bread,' she laughed, 'but why beans? As far as I can remember I've been served those darn kidney beans with every meal, morning noon and night. What is it with these people?'

'It's an old custom born of necessity. Beans and rice, or, if you prefer, rice and beans. It's the staple dish. It's like living in the deep South on the mainland—you get grits whether you order them or not.'

She dug in with a will, feeling a tremendous hunger. All due to excessive crying, she told herself. I must write a book about how to lose weight on a 'crybaby diet'. I might make a fortune.

'Are you telling yourself something important?' Jason queried.

'Are my lips moving again? It must be you. I've never had this trouble before!' She stifled a smile with a forkful of ham.

'You mean talking to yourself?'

'No,' she snapped. 'I always talk to myself. I mean moving my lips. That's something new.'

'You should have been a ventriloquist,' he suggested. She stared at him. Just sitting there looking at him was a sight. He was so—so assured. He looked as if he knew what he was going to do for the next fifty years, she thought. Confidence! I wish I had some of that!

'One of the things I'm going to do this summer is to take a class in lip-reading,' he drawled. 'There's nothing I hate worse than missing half the conversation. Are you ready to go?'

She gulped the last of her orange juice, stood up, and flipped her braids back over her shoulders. It hadn't seemed all that important to pin everything up. Not for a horseback ride.

'I like your hair that way,' he said softly. He was suddenly all the way around the table and close to her—too close. 'I think I would like it better if you let it hang loose. Where's your sombrero?'

'My *hat* is under my chair,' she snapped. For some reason his personal remarks irritated her. 'I wear my hair this way because *I* like it. Besides, I can't control it when it's loose. I think I shall have to get it cut one of these days real soon.'

He said something under his breath as he led the way out to the back patio. Evy wished with all her might for better hearing, but didn't dare to ask him to repeat what he had said, so she followed him down the hall, unabashedly admiring the way he moved, the panther-like motions of his shoulders, the swing of his trim slim hips, and the—and she bumped right into his back when he stopped just outside the door. He didn't say a word, just turned and looked down at her blush-red cheeks. There was a little gleam in his eye, but she was too inexperienced to interpret it.

Perdita was waiting for her again, the lovely big bay mare she had ridden on her first trip. Jason mounted a nervous black stallion that pranced and skittered as he put foot to stirrup. Nothing seemed to bother him. From that tremendous height he watched as Evy awkwardly manoeuvred her mount to the block which had been set up just for her. She managed to swing herself aboard— and not too shabbily at that, she told herself as she settled herself in the saddle.

'Here, take these.' He had been holding Perdita's reins. Now he passed them over to her. 'Both in one hand, like this.' He demonstrated. 'Now, sit back in the saddle. Forget all the riding school habits you ever read about. Sit back, enjoy the ride, and use your knees.'

'I—I'm to go by myself?' There was more than a little uneasiness in her voice.

'Not exactly alone,' he returned. 'The horse will go with you—all the time, I hope. And she's a lot smarter than you are about riding around the farm. Just relax.'

'Very funny,' she muttered. 'Very darn funny! It's a long way to fall from up here.'

'As long as you think of it that way, it shouldn't be too long before you *do* fall off. Try a little more positive thinking. Put your eyes on the horizon and let the horse watch the road.'

'Yes, Dr Freud,' she muttered under her breath.

'What was that?'

'I said yes, I hope you're not annoyed,' Evy lied blandly. 'Isn't it wonderful out here?' And indeed it was. Perdita followed daintily along in the footsteps of the stallion, acting as if butter would not melt in her mouth, and the outdoor world was suddenly at Evy's beck. It wasn't until she decided she would like to take a closer look at the coffee bushes, and tried to rein in, that the little mare demonstrated some intractability. The horse knew that her place was nose to tail with the stallion, and there she meant to stay, no matter what the almost weightless inconsequential rider had to say about it!

'How do I get her to stop?' Evy yelled after Jason. He reined in and looked around. 'Pull back evenly on the reins. Be firm—she has to know you're the boss.' She gave it a try. The bay stutter-stepped a couple of times, and continued plodding along.

'She has to believe you mean it,' he called. She glared at him. He had pulled up in the shade of some trees, freed one foot from the stirrup and coiled it around the horn of his saddle. And he was busily lighting a cigarette!

Evy pulled back on the reins again, with a little more force. 'Whoa,' she said gently, almost in the mare's ear. 'Whoa up, little darling.' There was no response. 'Damn you, horse,' she snarled, 'stop right here!' They had finally caught up to the stallion, waiting under the trees. The mare stopped short—short enough to throw Evy forward on to the saddle horn.

'Damn you!' she snapped again as she kicked both feet free of the stirrups and slid the impossible distance to the ground.

'See,' he said. 'You just have to be firm. Why did you want to get off here?'

'I didn't want to get off here,' she snapped. After all, it was his horse, and therefore his responsibility. 'I wanted to get off down there, and this—this animal wouldn't stop! You would think this was a bus route or something.

Only dismount at the approved stops! And it's your darn horse!'

'My, you look pretty when you're mad.' He was refusing all responsibility for the whole affair. 'Would you like to go on now?'

'I don't know.' She sighed wearily, damping her temper down. 'I—I don't think I can get back up there again. It's so—so high.'

'Easy.' He swung down from his saddle, leaving his mount on a ground loop, and walked over to her. She was not sure whether she ought to run, duck, or fight. And in the end she did nothing. He put both hands around her waist, spanning more than half the distance around with his huge fingers. He lifted her off her feet. She could feel a thrill at the sheer power in him. He's going to set me in the saddle, her mind told her. But that was his *second* intention. Before he made a move towards the saddle he held her suspended in air, her feet dangling loosely.

'Gotcha!' he grinned, and kissed her very gently but soundly. So by the time she was back in the saddle she was entirely out of breath, composure, and common sense. Lucky I'm sitting down, she told herself. If I wasn't I'd fall down! How does he do that to me? *Why* does he do that to me? What the devil does he think to accomplish in the middle of a coffee plantation—with only two horses to watch, and nobody within miles to—oh, lordy, what am I thinking! Francisca wouldn't like that! It bothered her so much that she told him so.

'Francisca? What does she have to do with anything? If she were here in your place she would probably enjoy it. Did you?'

The question came before she could get her guard up. 'Yes indeed,' her stupid tongue volunteered. But she was unable to leave it alone at just one mistake.

'Francisca probably would like it less if she knew that I enjoyed it,' she said primly.

'Probably,' he remarked. 'I must ask her some time.'

'I wish—I wish you wouldn't,' she returned, almost cringing at the thought. 'She's angry enough with me already. I don't think I could take much more!'

'So that's the reason you ran away last night! I thought it had something to do with the dinner!'

'Well, she's been very—very close to you, hasn't she?' For the life of her Evy could not bring herself to say 'engaged'. It was something important, that word—and she didn't *want* to know. At least not now.

'Yes. Francisca and I go a long way back. She and my sister Lucy were almost cradlemates. She was in and out of our house at all hours—underfoot relatives, my mother used to say. I've known her since she wore her first braces.'

'And loved her, I suppose?' The minute the words were out of her mouth she wanted to recall them. But that was impossible. So instead, she faced him boldly, her face smoothed into a stern but indifferent look—she hoped. That's another thing that orphans do, she told herself, school their faces to fit the situation.

'I hadn't given it much thought, but I suppose you're right,' said Jason as he urged his horse on up the hill. She followed him at a distance, allowing Perdita to choose the route. She had asked a foolish question, and got an answer she didn't want to hear, and that was all there was to that.

Their wandering path took them up and down the mountainside along the parallel rows of coffee bushes. Jason seldom dismounted, but often stopped to examine.

'What are you looking for?' she asked at last.

'Not much,' he replied. 'This is the flowering time. All we look for is healthy stems, quantity of flowers, condition of the leaf and petals, and bees. That's the important part—bees. Occasionally we have to spray, but things are looking good this year, so we may be able to cut down on the overhead.'

'I don't understand,' she confessed. 'Could you explain it to me again?'

'Why not?' They had come to the hump of the ridge, almost in the same spot where they had stopped the last time, by the bubbling spring that was the source of the river. Jason dismounted, helped Evy to do the same, and let the horses wander. 'They won't go far,' he promised her. 'I brought along some little something from the kitchen. Shall we have lunch up here?'

She looked around her. The ridge was not the highest point on the island, but from it there was an excellent view of the luxuriant land. 'You can hardly see where the little towns are, can you?' she asked in surprise.

'That's because they all have tree-lined streets,' he explained. 'Now, if we were to go over the mountains, and look down on the north side at all the big cities, it would be different. On the other side of the mountains it's all American Puerto Rico. On this side it's still Borinquen.'

'I don't understand.'

He looked at her seriously. 'Borinquen is the old Indian name for the island,' he told her. 'When you think of old-fashioned values, little towns, lots of green growth, you tend to think of it as Borinquen. On the other hand, there's modern up-to-date Puerto Rico, starting at San Juan and spreading through the industrialised area. When you think of that—well—'

'But everything has to change, doesn't it? You can't have the nineteenth-century Puerto Rico in the twentieth.'

'I don't know the answer,' he replied. 'Perhaps you're right. But you know how it goes. Man tries his

damnedest to make things good, and they turn out
badly. That's Puerto Rico. You ready for such serious
conversation?'

'I am if you're ready for a chicken salad sandwich?'
She handed out the contents of the basket which he had
carried strapped to his saddle.

'Okay,' he said moments later, as he munched. 'Go
back to this island before World War Two. Almost forty
per cent of the people lived off the land, and didn't do
very well. There was starvation, a high infant mortality,
little education, and plenty of malaria. So after the war,
when the island got its first native governor, it was
decided to try to industrialise. They called it Operation
Bootstrap. Industries were offered tax incentives and
government assistance to establish here. Many did,
especially petro-chemical plants. So the population living on the land dropped to twelve per cent. And then a
world-wide recession set in, the government, as planned, withdrew the tax incentives, and most of the
island's industry shut down. And that's where we are
today. Instead of having a rural unemployment mess,
we've got an industrial unemployment mess. Fifty per
cent of the population today receives a government
assistance subsidy. I can't begin to estimate how many of
the islanders have had to go north to the mainland to eke
out a living there. It's one hell of a mess.'

'And if you have to shut down the farm, there will be
that many more unemployed?'

'Yes, without a doubt. You know, sugar was once the
main money crop of the island. Today the only sugar
centrales working are owned by the government. They
keep them running at a loss just to provide mass employ-
ment. And the coffee *fincas* are not far behind. In fact,
only one of them made a profit last year. Well, settle for
today, and don't think about tomorrow.'

'I don't,' sighed Evy. 'I gave that up years ago. Just

think for today. Could you eat another sandwich?'

They finished off the lunch in good speed, then settled back in the soft bracken for siesta. I must really be getting to be a Puerto Rican, Evy told herself as her heavy eyelids closed under the shadow of her sombrero. The minute anyone says siesta, she thought, my eyes— and they did.

There was something peculiar about her awakening. Somehow or another her head was tilted up at an angle. She pushed back the brim of the big hat to look around. She was lying on the grass, as before, but her head was resting in Jason's lap. He was sitting up, toying with the loose strands of her silky hair. She started to sit up, but a hand on her shoulder held her down.

'Don't be in such a rush,' he said softly, so she settled back, willing to see what time would bring. It brought a flight of sparrows, the hoarse call of a macaw, the rustle of bamboo stands. Overhead, the sun flirted with the thin white clouds, dappling the landscape with patterns of light and shadow.

The scene and the scents and the time tipped her back into that half-shadowed world between sleep and awakening. She relaxed completely, slumping down to let her contours fit the earth on which she lay. But moments later she was shocked out of her dream. Jason's hand had moved from her shoulder, caressing her throat and ear-lobes, then it moved slowly and gently down to the declivity between her breasts. She held her breath, not sure what she should do next. There was no threat—yet. His warm fingers walked across the upper quarter of her sensitive globes, restrained by the drawstring that held her blouse closed. She struggled to control her ragged breathing, but the sensation continued, stirring ideas and memories she had long suppressed. She felt the tug as his other hand freed the drawstring, and her blouse fell away. She glued her eyes

shut, holding them together now by equal amounts of
panic and desire, and his hand marched on.

The single front clasp of her bra fell away, and now his
hand cupped her heavy breast, weighing it, exciting it.
Beyond her control the swelling mound hardened, the
nipple projecting like a proud pennant. His hand
marched up the hill, trapping the roseate peak between
thumb and forefinger. Riotous feelings coursed up and
down her spine, and she stiffened, arching upward
towards him. There was no way he could not know that
she was being stimulated. And with that came another
thought—of Frank, beside her in their bed, doing the
same things, looking towards the same goals—and she
remembered in violent colours what came afterwards.
When Jason's free hand tugged at the waistband of her
jeans, the memories exploded, and fear tore her away
from him, and sent her rolling down the hillside until
several feet separated them.

'What's the matter?' he asked bleakly as he sat and
watched her.

She fumbled with her clothes, rearranging them with
stiffened fingers. 'I—don't do that,' she stammered.

He covered the few feet, and was at her side. 'For
heaven's sake, Evy, you're a big girl now, and people do
this sort of thing. Don't you ever feel you want a man
again?'

She brushed his hand off violently and rolled away
from him. She struggled to her feet, her face flushed with
anger—and with fear. Jason moved towards her again,
but she backed cautiously away.

'What is it?' he snapped.

'It's you,' she retaliated. 'What is it with you men?
You think that just because I'm a widow I'm aching to
have some strong silent type bed me? Well, you've got
another think coming, Mr Brown! I don't want your
hands on me, or any other man's. If ever I feel the mad

urge to go to bed with someone, I'll pick him out for myself, thank you!' For just that moment, anger had overcome fear. She faced him like a clawing cat, wary of her ground, but willing to fight if driven to it.

'All right,' he grumbled, 'I've got the damn message. You don't have to hit me with a piledriver to make your point. I'll get the horses.'

She watched him carefully as he sauntered down the ridge a few feet to where the animals had found fresh grazing. By now her anger had cooled, and her fears were rising. To be all alone on a mountain with a man was problem enough; to be there with a man whom she had just rejected made a very serious problem. She could remember vividly the one time when she had rejected Frank. That was the time he had beat her down to the floor with his fists, and then kicked her, over and over again. It had brought a two-week hospital stay, and two broken ribs. And how she remembered it!

Jason came up the hill leading the horses and passed her the reins without a word. She did her best to turn the animal on the downward side of the hill, to get a little extra advantage, but even that was not enough to allow her to mount. She was trying for the third time when unexpectedly his hand grabbed her heel and threw her up in the air. She landed in the saddle, but it was a matter of luck rather than skill, and the sudden flight through the air was enough to trigger a major reaction. She was screaming while in the air. When she landed in the saddle she seized the saddle horn and a handful of Perdita's mane, and continued to scream the world down.

It was too much for the bay mare. As amiable as one could ever expect, Perdita was not prepared for a sudden screeching assault. She reared, something she had not done in years, and before Jason could react, the horse bolted.

There was nothing Evy could do but hang on. She bent forward in the saddle, grabbing more of the mare's flowing mane, trying desperately to get her feet into the stirrups. And all the while she was adding to the confusion of the flight by screaming. The two runaways quickly cleared the top of the ridge and plunged into the shadows of the plantation. Now there were added dangers. The ground underfoot was soft, and the branches of the shade trees stretched over everything. They fled downhill like a wild juggernaut, completely out of control. Behind them the black stallion hammered along, its rider spurring it into the trees, and cursing at the top of his lungs.

Twice the fleeing mare stumbled in her mad rush, but managed to recover her feet. Through it all Evy was shaking with a fear not imaginable to the man behind her. It was not just the runaway mount, it was the sexual attack, the long nights of worry, the long years of hatred, and the memories that could not be stilled, no matter what. She fought off the attacks on her mind as long as she could, but eventually she cracked. The sweetly haunted blonde beauty of an hour before became a mindless thing, clutching herself to the back of the horse like a limpet on its host, her screams inaudible now except to Jason, for Evy's mind had fled the horror.

As a result, when the bay came to a feverish halt five hundred feet down the mountainside, and bucked its rider off into the bushes, Evelyn Hart was not there to feel the pain.

Jason brought the black stallion up behind her not seconds later, vaulting off his mount without pause, and running the last few paces to where she lay in a crumpled heap on the ground. He ran anxious but experienced hands over her body, noting the awkward break in her hand, measuring the concussion, and counting the scratches that spread a red curtain down the side of her face. Careful of her hand, he picked her up in his arms and looked around.

The bay, her troubles over, had gone on down the mountain to the barn. The black stood waiting patiently under the shade of the coffee bushes, flanks still heaving from the speed of the dangerous ride. Jason whistled, and the horse responded to his call. He held the girl close for a time, examining the damage to his precious vessel, and felt a murderous instinct in his heart against himself. Manoeuvring carefully to avoid further damage to the hand, he managed to lay her over the saddle, then swung himself up behind.

The trip back to the house was slow, and after he was securely mounted he picked her up in his arms to save her from the inevitably rough trip. Alerted by the return of the bay, men were standing by at the stable to help. They came out on the run, and helped Jason down with his load, but he refused to surrender her, even though there were fresher arms available.

Maria was attracted by the noise, and met them at the door. Her old head had suffered through many an incident such as this. She crossed herself, and sped off ahead of him to get a bed ready, splashing voluble Spanish commands around the house like a sprinkling of holy water.

Jaime was the cool hand who did the work. He called the doctor, threatening him with death and instant disbarment if he failed to appear at once, and dispatching the helicopter and its half-awake pilot to make sure the trip was accomplished.

They managed to get Evy to her own bed, gently stripped her, and washed her cuts and bruises. 'There's a simple fracture of that bone in her hand,' Jason told Jaime as Maria fussed. 'Lay it out on the pillow until the doctor arrives. I'll sit with her until then. You will have somebody see to the horses, *amigo*?'

'*Seguro, patrón*,' answered Jaime and left the bedroom. As he went out the back door his eye caught a movement in the living room, and he stopped. Francisca de Molinaro was standing next to the table, the telephone in her hand. There was a very complacent smile on her face as she talked, but the moment she caught sight of Jaime at the door, she cut off her conversation, put the telephone down, and smiled at him.

'Mrs Hart is not hurt too badly?' she asked.

'She's in shock,' he reported grimly. 'Perhaps a broken hand, some cuts and bruises. Do you really care?'

'Why, of course I do, *querido*,' she laughed. 'I care very much. Now Jason will be inconvenienced more than ever!'

'What are you scheming at?' he asked softly. 'You know that Jason was never for you. But I am waiting. You need me, Francisca, not those clowns you deal with in San Juan.'

'Oh, really?' She measured him up and down, as she had done many times before. 'Perhaps you could be right, Jaime. But only perhaps.'

He turned away to continue his errand, shaking his head as he went. Francisca dropped on to the divan, lit up a cigarette, and laughed as she had not laughed for years. Her clear bell tones even reached the bedroom, but Evy Hart did not care at all.

CHAPTER SIX

SHE had fallen into a deep well, and there was no way out. There was a gleam of light in the distance, like a small sun glaring down at her, but her hands and feet scrabbled at the sidewalls of the well and could find no purchase. Every few minutes she tried to scramble out, only to fall back to the bottom, crying. I must get out, she told herself, but she knew it was impossible. She was trapped for ever. Occasionally a shadow would fall over her world, and she would sense a presence. She cried out feebly when she felt it, until a pin pricked her arm and brought blessed oblivion.

On the third day she climbed to that realm of consciousness just below full recall, where the psyche knows, but cannot control. She drifted in this layer for a day and a night, feeling no pain, having no command over her body, but hearing what went on around her. She knew when the doctor came into the room, usually accompanied by a roar of anger in Jason's familiar voice. She knew when Maria bustled nearby, half-singing the old island tunes of her youth.

And finally she came to that level where she was completely in control, but commanded her eyes to remain closed, for fear of what she might see. Her body was healing itself, but her mind refused to come out of hiding. Until he drove her out.

She felt the pressure on her hand as she gradually awoke. Peeping under the tiniest corner of one eyelid, she could see the sun lighting the room with perpetual tropical brightness. Jason was sitting on the edge of a chair close beside the bed, her left hand clasped between both of his. She slammed her eye shut.

'You can't hide out in the open,' he said, tugging at her hand. Evy commanded her body not to respond, but there was an itchy feeling around her nose, as if some tiny insect were tracing its way up from tip to base. Despite her command to freeze, her nose wrinkled. 'It's impossible to deceive me,' he said in a melodramatic voice. She popped one eye open. He was leaning over her, too close for comfort, using a little feather to tickle her.

'That's not fair,' she grumbled, trying to swat his hand away with her own free one. She was unaware until then of the heavy cast on her right hand, and it banged into him with a thud. 'Oh, my heavens, what have I done? Are you all right?'

'I don't think so,' he mourned. 'I shall probably be scarred for life.'

'That will leave a bruise, not a scar,' she retorted primly.

'Well, whatever, it's got you talking again,' he laughed. 'The doctor says you've been faking for the past twelve hours. Is that true?'

'None of your business,' she snapped, and was instantly seized with contrition. 'I didn't mean that,' she stammered, searching desperately for a change of subject. 'How is Perdita?'

'Ah! Change into the fast lane, huh? Perdita is fine. She was back in the barn before you and I started down the hill. Now, how about you? How come you were turning us all off?'

'I—' she stammered, not knowing what to say. Wouldn't it be nice, she thought, to be able to tell someone everything, without censorship, without forming and tasting each sentence before it was delivered. And why not Jason? There was nobody else in the world whose opinion she cherished. Why not him?

'I—I want you to know something about me.' She started off in a rush, in a hurry to get the words out. 'I—you must realise what a coward I am. Once, when I'd been hurt badly and was terribly frightened, I—they—took me to a—to a hospital. And—'

'To a mental hospital?'

'Yes. To the state psychiatric hospital. I—I had what they called a—breakdown. I couldn't face people—or things. And they took me in, and—I spent three months there. I was so ashamed of what I'd done to Frank—and I just couldn't face anybody. Do you understand what I'm trying to say.' She looked over at him with large pleading eyes.

'I understand, Evy. You had one hell of a shock, and you had a nervous breakdown. It happens to lots of people. And it isn't terribly important, only I can see that it left you super-sensitive to life, didn't it?'

'Yes, it did. I try to fight it—but sometimes—'

'And that's what happened up on the mountain, didn't it? I pushed you too far, and you had a flashback, and just withdrew from the world again?'

'Yes, I—what you said. I frightened that poor horse half to death, for no good reason at all except that I was—frightened—myself. Without cause! You must think me some sort of nincompoop, some sort of idiot child—don't you?' For the first time Evy opened both eyes and looked directly at him. There was no reproach in him. In fact he looked as if he understood what she meant. He looked—lovable.

'You had plenty of cause,' he commented. 'I got carried away. Can I tell you something serious, Evy?'

'Yes, if you wish.'

'I want you so badly I can taste it, Evy Hart. Does that surprise you?'

'I—no—please, don't talk to me that way. I'm not up on the auction block. I—you—' What can I tell him? she thought. That men frighten me? He knows that already, but not to what depth. He thinks he can charm me up out of my doldrums. I want you! Just what Frank once said. I want you! And look what that led to. Dear God, I want him too, but I dare not have him. For my life, I dare not have him!

She tried to move away from him on the bed, only to have her muscles scream so much that it brought tears to her eyes. Jason settled back in his chair, watching, as she began to take some account of her problems, tried to shut out what he had said.

There was a heavy cast on her right hand, extending out to her wrist. A bandage covered part of her head, the left section of her forehead. Some of her hair had been cut away to make room for it, her exploring hand told her. There were furrows on her cheek, too, as if long narrow scratches had finally begun to heal. And beyond that, she ached all over.

'Don't worry about it,' said Jason. 'Your head and face will be totally healed in a week or so. It's only the hand that might give trouble for a longer time. You have what the doctor called a greenstick fracture of one of the small bones. And you have some mountain-size bruises on your—er—on your bottom. But that will all pass away, or I'll have that damn doctor's tonsils bare-handed. Now, two pills every four hours. Can you swallow lying down?'

'Not without choking to death,' she managed to get out. He smiled sympathetically, and helped her into a semi-sitting position, propped up by extra pillows. The pills looked tiny, felt enormous in her dry throat, and went down only after generous applications of cool orange juice. Jason helped her to lie flat again, brushed a kiss over her forehead, and went out of the room.

I need to be more rational about this, she told herself. He wants me. Well, I knew that right from the beginning. And now I know the corollary. I want him. So why don't I just grab him and run? Francisca would be angry, but so what? Maria would probably be offended too. But what exactly does he want? He hasn't said 'marriage', and I don't think I'm ready to listen to a proposal anyway. How about that? Straitlaced Evelyn Hart—I don't mind his proposition, but I can't abide his proposal! Well, there's nothing I can do about it now. But as long as I'm lying here building up my strength, I might as well build up my courage too, and then we'll see! There was such a satisfied expression spread across her face when the pills dropped her off into the canyon of darkness that Jason stopped to admire more than once, when he should have been tied up in his communications room, managing an empire.

She awoke again just as the clocks in the house struck noon. Francisca was sitting by the bed, leafing through an old copy of *Vogue* magazine. Evy stirred, and immediately drew the other woman's attention.

It was the start of a week of small attentions. Francisca appeared daily in the sickroom, willing to do the slightest errand, and filling in the empty hours by gossip, mostly about fashions. Evy was surprised at first, and then grateful. With the gradual return of her strength the hours were getting longer and longer. It was beyond her experience that someone would be kind to her in a sickbed, and the fact that the sophisticated Spanish girl would become a sickroom attendant was a considerable ego-builder. So amazed was she at the change in Francisca's deportment that she hardly noticed, in the doing, that Jason and Maria were being shut out of the sickroom by those same manoeuvres. It took Maria's sharp comments to bring it to the fore.

'But it must save you thousands of steps,' protested Evy. 'She seems willing to do so many things. I don't quite know what to make of it all.'

'What steps it should save?' Maria was busy re-making the bed with fresh linen, while Evy enjoyed an hour in a comfortable chair by the window. 'I am only here to take care of you, *mariposa*. Is not so hard a job, no? And I see that the Señorita comes in your room only when *El Jefe* is in the house. You notice this? When he is out in the plantation, this woman is hard to find. But when he returns, always she is in here. When does he get a time to be alone with you?'

'Why, I—I never thought of that,' Evy replied. Her mind went spinning with this new concept. I thought he—he didn't want to be alone with me, that he didn't come because—oh, I don't know! You must think me a fool, Maria.'

'No.' The busy hands continued picking up the room, readjusting the curtains, smoothing the blanket thrown over Evy's knees. 'Young, perhaps. It is a puzzle. There is a revolution of the sexes in the world, my grand-children tell me. But instead of *more* knowledge, you have so much less than I did when I was your age. About men, I mean. You act like a little virgin just out of the convent. Where is the Señorita today?'

'She went down to the Playa for me. I was getting so restless, she volunteered to go down and get my drawing materials, so I could go back to work. Wasn't that nice?'

'She has the keys to the house?'

'Of course. How else would she get the materials?'

'But she left early this morning? She has her own car. A trip of thirty minutes, no? And already it is four o'clock in the afternoon. Besides, how do you make the drawings with a broken hand?'

'It's my right hand that's broken, silly. You know that I'm left-handed.'

'Ah! How could I forget? Yes, of course. Everything will be all right. I am being an old worrier, no?' The elderly woman bustled for a few minutes more, emptied the trash baskets, left a few words of encouragement, and walked out of the room. And that night, when her grandson Ramón came for a social visit, she lost no time at all in repeating the entire conversation to his very attentive ear.

Beginning the next morning, Evy was allowed out of bed for four hours at a time. The receipt of her drawing materials had been a godsend, but no amount of concentration could bring her back to the tiny world of Sylvester the Seal, so she took herself out to the veranda and sketched everything in sight. Charcoal sketches they were, more caricature than real life. There were a tumbling pair of mongooses who lived in a hollow just below the lily pond. Before the second day was out, Evy had developed them into a family, with a multitude of problems that could make a good story-line for a completely new cartoon. But the moment she realised what she was doing she abandoned the mongooses and turned to real people. Francisca filled many pages, mostly because she was the one readily available. Despite Maria's scepticism, Evy had developed an affection for the Spanish girl, and a sort of trust grew up between them.

But during those times when Francisca disappeared, Evy found her hand unconsciously producing sketches of Jason. Jason in formal dinner clothes. Jason in informal, boyish moods. Jason with stars in his eyes. Her only problem was to keep the drawings out of sight of the subject himself—no easy task, that, since he had taken up the habit of dropping in on her unexpectedly, no matter what the hour. Their meetings were always pleasant. After the first few, she came to accept his quiet presence, his casual conversation, and the occasional light touch of his hand on her shoulder, or running lightly through her hair.

When Francisca was present—which *did* seem very

often—he left the conversation to the two women. When he was alone, he became a fountain of information, gossip, small jokes. Until suddenly Evy discovered that she missed him when he failed to show up. She marked that knowledge down in her heart, and did her best not to make an outward show of it.

By the second week of her convalescence she was fully mobile, although her hand was still in the cast. Most of the bruises on her shoulder and on her thighs had progressed through shades of blue to green and yellow, and then had faded away. The long scratches on her face had healed completely, and the cut on the side of her head was now covered with a downy fuzz as her hair began to grow back. And best of all, she noticed one morning, as she changed out of her nightgown, her ribs no longer stuck out like a shipwrecked hulk, and her bony hip projections were becoming sleek and curvaceous. 'All due to your four meals a day, Maria,' she chuckled as she dressed.

'We should celebrate,' Francisca said one afternoon. 'How about if we go into Santiago tomorrow and go shopping? There's no better way to restore your health than a good shopping trip!'

It sounded just right. 'I do need some few things,' Evy agreed. 'Some cosmetics, some unmentionables—oh, and just a change of scenery! Tomorrow, about nine o'clock? I'd love to take a trip like that.'

'A trip like what?' Jason came out on to the veranda to join them, followed by Maria with a tray of cold drinks.

'Oh, Evy wants to go into the town,' Francisca reported. 'She's bored out here in the country. So I thought I could drive her in, and we would spend the morning shopping.'

Jason sipped at his glass, and looked at Evy with those piercing eyes. Why does it sound so different when she says it? Evy asked herself. All of a sudden it's *my* idea, because *I'm* bored! I would have bet that *she's* the one who is bored. She's more out of place on a farm than I am.

'Is that true, Evy?' That little white tuft of eyebrow was standing straight up in the air, giving him a more devilish look than ever.

'Well, it would be a nice change,' she said softly. The supple fingers of her left hand were hard at work sketching him. There was a difficulty capturing his facial expression. She had thrown away dozens of attempts, but this one looked successful. She smiled to herself and nibbled at the end of her pencil. He walked around behind her chair and looked over her shoulder before she could take precautions.

'Why, you little devil!' His warm voice was just at her ear. 'Is that how you really see me? The fallen Lord, Satan?'

Evy looked down at her own handiwork, as much startled as he. And of course he was right. She had given him the sweetly seductive face of the fallen angel! 'Oh no,' she laughed, sweeping her heavy eraser over the face of the sketch, 'I don't think of you that way at all!' No, I don't. I wouldn't dare!

'About the trip,' interrupted Francisca, and Jason looked over at her as if considering something other than shopping trips.

'No—not really. The prime reason for keeping Evy here is to protect her. A shopping trip to Santiago is out of the question.' He tipped up his glass in a toast to them all, while Francisca fumed.

'It's only a shopping trip,' she protested. 'And who in the world would be interested in some—in Mrs Hart?'

'We don't know that yet,' he said. 'That's why she's not going. But there's no reason why you can't go if you want to. Jaime said earlier that he needed to go into town for a number of things. Why don't you go with him?'

'If I wanted to go with him I would have asked him!' Francisca set her drink down on the end table with an emphatic thump and almost ran back into the house.

'I certainly put my foot in my mouth that time, didn't I?' he asked ruefully. 'Do you suppose she'll ever forgive me?'

There was something—sarcastic—in the tone he used, almost as if he enjoyed the swift interchange. I just don't understand him, Evy told herself. He's engaged to the girl. She's a beautiful creature. And sometimes he acts as if she were part of the furniture! In a way I'm glad it's not me he's engaged to—but then do I really mean that? Maybe he—

'Talking to yourself again?' he asked. He came over beside her and joined her on the divan. Somehow or another the relatively large piece of furniture seemed to have shrunk. He barely squeezed himself in, forcing his warm thigh up against her lightly covered leg. Evy did her best to move away from the close contact, but there was nowhere to more. Sit still, she commanded her trembling body. Sit still. He doesn't have to affect you like some simpering High School girl!

Despite all her commands, she almost jumped out of her skin when his hand dropped to her knee. Don't react, she screamed at herself. That's what he wants. He's only teasing. Don't react!

'Something bothering you?' He sounded as casual as if his hand were resting on a marble statue, rather than sending wild surges of panic up her spine.

'I—no.' Damned if I'll let him see me panic, she told herself. But it wasn't all that easy. His other arm had been draped along the back of the divan, and now it moved down on to her shoulder, with disastrous results as far as her nerves were concerned. She stirred uneasily, as the hand came down on her shoulder and fixed her in place. It was too much, but this time she had control of herself. It would never again be as it had been on the mountain, with her jumping away, out of control, in a complete panic.

'I—I wish you wouldn't do that,' she said softly, refusing to meet his eyes.

The hand on her knee withdrew. The one on her shoulder remained, squeezing her gently, then caressing her upper arm. 'Please,' she repeated. Jason's sigh echoed through the area like a warning wind. He got up and replenished his glass, staring out over the lily pond all the while.

'Too soon?' he asked.

'Yes,' she mourned. 'A year too soon. A lifetime too soon—I don't know. Maybe it's an eternity of wrongness. I can't help it, Jason. You must have me as I am, or I must go back home.'

'That sounds nice,' he returned. There was a harshness in the little laugh that accompanied the words. 'I'd be glad to have you any way I can get you.'

'I—I didn't mean that,' she stammered. 'I wish you wouldn't always misinterpret what I say. I—'

Whatever it was she had planned to say became superfluous, for Ramón came out on to the veranda, followed by Maria. Jason welcomed them as if he too had found the conversation getting over his head.

'*Que tal, amigo?*'

'Everything goes well,' Ramón responded. 'Too slowly for Abuela, but fast enough by police standards! I'll have anything to drink so long as it's rum.'

'Such manners!' his grandmother commented. '*Sientate*. I will bring the drinks.' She bustled over to the bar and began to mix the rum and Coke combination. 'And you, *linda*?'

'Lemonade,' she responded automatically. The detective sank down into one of the upholstered chairs and stretched his feet out in front of him.

'I thought we had a nibble today,' he sighed, toasting them with his glass. 'One of the teachers in the school at the Playa reported someone in your house. We rushed down, of course, and found your Miss Molinaro inside looking for something. A false alarm, of course. Strange—the neighbours reported that there was a man with her, but we couldn't find him. Must have been a mistake.'

'Must have been,' contributed Jason. 'You didn't get your keys back from Francisca when she went down for your art materials, Evy?'

'Why—no, I guess I didn't. Is it important?'

'Perhaps not.' He seemed unable to keep his eyes off the garden, where the local family of mocking birds were creating a small riot. Look at me, Evy commanded silently. Look at me! But he continued to stare at the birds.

'But I do have something concrete to mention,' the detective continued. 'There seem to be an unusually large number of strangers in the district during the past three days. Half a dozen or so, my people tell me, and some of them Cubans.'

'Come on now,' Jason admonished him. 'That's the same as saying "It must have been outsiders who did it!" You can't blame everything on Cubans. There are a lot of very respectable people in the Cuban community.'

'I don't understand,' interrupted Evy. 'What Cubans? Why?'

'It's a local argument,' Jason told her. 'After Castro took over in Cuba, a good many of the Cuban middle-class came to Puerto Rico instead of Miami. They set themselves up in business. They work hard, and ninety nine per cent of them are honest, hard-working people. But along with them came some of the gamblers, the mobsters, who once operated the gambling concessions in Havanna. And they're looking for a foothold here.'

'It is the official position of the government that there are no Cuban mobsters operating in this island,' Ramón commented.

'Give a dog a bad name?' asked Evy. 'In Cleveland everyone thinks that if you have an Italian name you must be with the Mafia. And that's not true, either.'

'Stay for dinner,' invited Jason. 'You might as well. It's getting towards six o'clock already.'

'Dinner is not until seven o'clock,' Maria said sternly.

'Come on,' Jason laughed. 'You're such a snob, Doña Maria. Neither Evy or I object to eating dinner with a policeman. And we certainly don't object to sharing a meal with your grandson!'

It all made an interesting evening, with sparkling conversation and laughter. That was, everyone but Francisca found it to be an interesting evening. She sat in her usual place, to Jason's left, and hardly a word passed her compressed lips. Shortly after they adjourned for coffee Miss Molinaro made her excuses and drove off in the night, at the wheel of her sporty little BMW. 'She acts as if someone has twisted her tail,' mused Jason as they watched the tail lights recede down the mountain.

Evy went to bed early, after all that. Or rather, she was sent to bed early. She found it difficult to laugh and yawn at the same time, until finally Maria commented as she bustled in with fresh coffee. After which Jason insisted—like the darn dictator he is, Evy told herself, and off she went.

It had been a long, tiring, exciting day. She wrapped a plastic bag around her cast, enjoyed a long hot shower, towelled herself clumsily with her one hand, and climbed into bed. On the verge of sleep, she recalled the day. Jason had gone from boyish friend to careful adviser, to dictator. Each hour of the day brought change.

Will the real Jason Brown please stand up? The idea brought a giggle, which she promptly hid under the soft blanket on the bed. And those hands—those roaming, teasing hands! Why had she not objected sooner? Because they weren't objectionable, her prim little conscience reminded her.

Jason's hands on her body had been—interesting. And she had only objected out of past habit, not present desire. There was the key word—desire. He wants me; I want him. A simple equation for happiness—even if only for a short time! He's obviously not in any great hurry to marry Francisca. Perhaps that's it? He wants enough time to play around with just one more bird before he has to pack it all in? And I wouldn't mind being that pigeon—if only I can keep up my courage and make the first hurdle! she told herself. .

And wouldn't that make Francisca's head spin? Like wow! If that woman knew what I'm thinking right now she'd be around in the middle of the dark of night with an axe, Evy mused, no, not an axe. Women don't kill with an axe. A poison pill? A hypodermic loaded with air? Or maybe she would just stab me to death with her eyes! But she's been so good to me these last two weeks. All the little things, the tiny services that makes sickbed life livable. No, perhaps Francisca isn't as bad as I first thought. And here I am scheming to steal her man away from her! Why don't I feel contrite? Imagine her giving Jason the idea that I wanted to leave the farm, when all the time it was her own idea? Oh well, it can't be important. Why did she go back to my house in the Playa? And on that note Evy pulled the blanket up to her chin, wiggled herself down in the bed, and dropped off.

She was up early for breakfast, and so was Jason. They ate out in the shade by the lily pond. The day was newly washed by an early-morning shower, but the garden had quickly dried under the tropical sun. The mocking birds were at it again, noisy, friendly, imitative.

'Are these the only birds on the island?' she asked as one of the younger ones dive-bombed their table.

'Hard to tell,' he said. 'There are several other birds of the thrasher family living on the island. And plenty of cow-birds. You don't see them much around her because they follow the cattle. Oh, and owls, two or three types. A few parakeets—not too many of them. When I was young we all used to go out trapping parakeets and parrots. We made spending money out of it. But that's all stopped. The parrots are a real native strain, on the endangered species list now. They only nest up in the rain forest. And that's about it. The island has no real indigenous wild life, you know—except for the wild boars. Whatever there once was, along with the Indians who lived off them, all are long gone.'

'You mean there's no Indian blood in Puerto Rico?'

'Oh, perhaps a little, but not much. Most of the Indians were wiped out within seventy or eighty years of the first Spanish occupation.'

'There's one good thing about it, then. There's nothing dangerous living out in the forest?'

'Plenty of dangerous things,' he returned. 'There's man, and there's the scorpion. They're both deadly!'

Delfinia broke up the discussion. 'It calls you,' she announced, sticking just her head out the screen door. 'The radio.'

'My master's voice,' said Jason. He was smiling as he got up from the little folding table, dropped the napkin, and started up the stairs towards his office.

'And what do I do?' Evy yelled after him. There was more than a little disappointment in her voice.

'Come along with me,' he called back. But he didn't stop.

'Come along with me,' she repeated to the mocking

birds. 'Damn! And why not?' She gulped down the last
of her coffee, and stood up to follow. There was just one
tiny bite of ham left on the serving tray. With almost a
guilty feeling she looked around to make sure she was
unobserved, then snapped it up. She munched happily
as she sauntered up the path. Four more weeks of this,
girl, she lectured herself, and you'll need a whole new
wardrobe. Everything fits tightly! And the things that
used to fit tightly, they don't fit at all. But it's all going to
the right places, she noted as she admired herself in the
glass of the door. A little more padding on the hips is
required—not much, just a little. And there's already
been a nice increase over the shoulder bones and
breasts!

'You shouldn't talk to yourself like that, *linda*,' said
Maria as they passed in the corridor. 'You starting to
behave like girl who eats too much, no? Or maybe needs
a man. Oh, what I have say!' And the *dueña* hurried by
on her way to the kitchen.

'Maria!' Evy was momentarily shocked at the comment, but then her good humour triumphed, and she
turned into the radio room laughing, while Maria trotted
downstairs whooping in her surprisingly strong
contralto.

When Evy turned to look, the room silenced her. She
had always felt a tremendous respect—and fear—of
technology, and the room was full of it. From floor to
ceiling electronic equipment gleamed at her. Jason was
sitting in the middle of the room, at a semi-circular
console. Two other young men whom she had not
previously met were working in the corner, servicing
equipment.

'So you did come!' He sounded very satisfied—almost
smug—as he waved her over to his imposing position.
Why, he looks just like a little boy with a new electric
train! she thought. That was the first impression, and the

second—why, I never realised how handsome he is! She walked over to him slowly, requiring time to stabilise her thoughts.

'What do you think?' he asked, waving a hand at the conglomeration of lights blinking on and off.

'I don't know,' she confessed. 'I thought you tycoons always had a dozen secretaries at your elbow, all prepared to kowtow, and do whatever secretaries do.'

He grinned broadly at her. 'I do have a couple. They work in our office in San Juan. I just don't need to share space with them any more.'

'So that's the wave of the future,' she teased him. 'You don't need women in your office any more. How on earth do you run things?'

'The principal job a secretary performs,' he pontificated, 'is to find information for me, so I can make decisions. And then they write down my orders. Now, all I do is ask the computer. Of course we have a dozen people in the city who keep feeding information into the monster, but I ask all my questions from here. I get more information, faster, and in the form I want it, than ever before. Neat?'

'Oh, neat,' laughed Evy, perching idly on the edge of his console with one foot still on the floor. 'But does the computer smell nice? Or bring you hot coffee? Or smile at you when you're down in the dumps?'

Jason looked up at her quizzically. 'Don't underestimate the power of the electron,' he said solemnly. 'And in the end, I send my instructions to the computer, which sends them along by satellite circuits, to whomever needs it. And presto, we make another half million!'

Be a devil, her inner conscience told her. Stir up this chauvinist smug man! And why not? She leaned closer to him, allowing the soft fullness of her hair to fall over his face. 'Don't underestimate the power of Chanel Number Five,' she said softly, and as seductively as she could.

'Why, damn you, Evy Hart,' he laughed; 'are you trying to blow the fuses on my computer?'

'No,' she confessed amiably. 'Just in you!'

She had meant at this point to duck and run, but he was too quick for her. She was suddenly enveloped in those strong arms of his, pulled off her perch on to his lap, and fixed in position. Overwhelmed, in dazed awe, she remained frozen in position as his head came down on her, shutting out all the light. And then his lips brushed against hers, shutting off her will to resist. He increased the pressure, just enough to force her lips open, and just enough to destroy all her reserve, all her pent-up emotions, and send her moaning against him, her good arm wrapped around his neck in a death grip, body squirming to get closer to him. The pressure continued, and the sensations shooting through her mind sent shivers down her spine. Until they both ran out of breath, and he put her gently aside, setting her on her feet.

The two servicemen were standing in the corner watching them, eyes as big as saucers, tools down on the floor.

'Well, Evy Hart,' gasped Jason, struggling out of his swivel chair, 'you sure pick one hell of a time! Wow!'

Wow indeed! What *have* you done, Evy Hart? she asked herself. Her face turned bright red, and she was still tingling and shaking from the impact—of just one kiss! What have you done, Evy Hart! Both hands flew to her embarrassed face as she turned and ran out of the room and farther—into the garden and up the mountain, out of sight.

CHAPTER SEVEN

The *finca* was large, as such island farms go, but hardly large enough for Evy to hide from Jason all day. Besides, she told herself disconsolately, I've walked as far as my feet will carry me, and I'm hungry. As a result, still berating herself, she stumbled through the coffee plantation and managed to find the house at about two o'clock in the afternoon.

'*Ay Madre de Dios!*' Maria exclaimed as Evy stumbled up the front steps. 'What you have done to you? Just look—holes in you skirt, leafs in you hair! And out walking in siesta. What?'

'Don't fuss, Maria,' Evy pleaded, 'there's a good girl. I had to—I just went for a walk, and now I'm hungry.'

'Ah!' That at least was a problem whose solution was ready at hand. While Evy sought refuge in her bathroom, combing out her hair and restoring her clothing, Maria concocted a calorie-laden lunch.

'So eat, *linda*. The chicken especially. It will make you more—what is the word?'

'Fat!' Evy laughed up at the elderly woman, and gratefully accepted the invitation. In fact, she gorged herself on the golden quarters of batter-fried chicken, and managed to finish the beautifully arranged salad which accompanied it. After lunch, feeling more at ease in her world, she picked up her sketchbook and pencils and went back out on to the veranda, determined more than ever to capture a good impression of the family of birds that seemed to own the garden. She had unannounced company. No sooner had she set to work when she heard movement overhead, and looked up.

110

'Oh, you, Pedro!' She had lost her fear of the family gecko, now peering down at her from the rafters. It had been helped by her discovery that almost every bedroom in the house had its own little chameleon, whose business was also insect-hunting. But although the chameleons changed colours with aplomb, they lacked the panache that Pedro possessed. When the bigger lizard spotted prey, in flight or still, its eyes would track the insect for a moment as if challening it to escape, then that long prehensile tongue would snap out with utmost precision, and remove the offender with a flourish.

So, taking advantage of the model, Evy added Pedro to the list of personalities to be sketched, and was busily engaged in that endeavour when Jason and Jaime came out on to the porch. They continued their argument as they came. Both went directly to the corner bar, and were filling tall glasses before they noticed that she was there, half hidden by the tall back of the chair she was using.

'*Hola*, Señora Hart,' Jaime called out, raising a glass to entice her. 'Would you like a drink?'

She nodded, concentrating on the last little detail of Pedro's tail. As usual, when she worked, her tongue was clenched between her lips, its tip barely protruding. When her pencil had added the last precise line she relaxed. 'Lemonade,' she requested. Jaime filled another glass for her, while Jason came around beside her chair to look at the work in progress.

'Pedro!' he announced, as if making some big discovery, and for just a second she felt like hitting him. 'I thought you were a cartoonist,' he continued, 'and here you are a nature-life painter.'

'Not really,' she returned, unable to repress the strange feelings that ran up and down her spine the moment he came close to her. Patronising, she told herself, that's what he is. Patronising. Oh, are you really a painter? House or picture? Damn the man! Why does he excite me so?

'I'm not a painter,' she snapped. 'I'm sketching.' She dropped her pencil into the little holder on her sketch-book and slammed it shut.

'Hey, there's no need to get huffy about it,' he replied, and that damnable hand dropped on to her shoulder again. She shrugged away from it, and started to get up. 'No need to move,' Jason said gruffly. 'I can take the hint. You're strictly a morning person, right?' He moved over to the divan and sat down. Evy dropped back into her chair and glared at him—at his back, really. He had turned away from her and taken up the argument with Jaime.

'But you saw the results they got,' insisted Jaime. 'A twenty per cent saving in labour costs, which were just enough to make the farm profitable.'

'Perhaps.' Jason was not about to give in so easily. 'Let's ask a third party. Evy?'

'If you're talking about coffee, I still don't know beans about it,' she snapped. They both stared at her, that disdainful stare on their faces that people produce when they hear a particularly bad pun. 'I wasn't trying to be funny,' she growled.

'Okay,' chuckled Jason, 'it was a little bit funny, at that. But listen to the problem. Are you ready?'

She nodded, folding her hands in her lap and trying her best to look cool and intelligent.

'There's a farm up the way where they've tried a new idea for coffee picking,' he told her. 'That's where the great expense is. The coffee beans ripen at different times, and must be picked when ripe. It takes a great deal of labour. So this fellow has surrounded all his bushes with nets. He lets the berries ripen at their own speed, and occasionally a team goes up the line shaking the bushes. The ripe berries fall off into the nets, then all his people have to do is empty the nets. The berries get a little more bruising, but it doesn't hurt the bean inside. How about that?'

'It sounds very practical,' she returned, 'that is, if you have to cut jobs. So what's your problem?'

'Two problems. First of all, the birds treat the whole affair as a free lunch. Second, there's still a considerable amount of labour involved in setting and emptying the nets.'

'What's the bottom line?'

'Last year he made a profit—the only coffee *finca* on the island to do so.'

Evy's fingers had automatically returned to pencil and sketchbook, and she laughed as she worked. The two men stared at her, but her head was bobbing as she drew, providing a shelter of swirling hair behind which she hid. 'You don't have an opinion?' prodded Jason.

'Oh, I have an opinion,' she returned demurely, 'but it—well, if the only way you can save some of the jobs is by closing down others—damn, that just goes against my principles. No, I guess I don't have an opinion. If the idea keeps the farm going, you ought to give it a try. Unless it's copyrighted?'

'So what's so funny?'

'It's—well, you would never understand. You have to live in the world of cartooning to—I—it's nothing.'

'You mean your cartoon hero would have a solution?'

'Well, of course. But that doesn't mean that it's necessarily practical in the real world,' she admitted. 'A cartoon hero can solve anything.'

'So tell us,' Jaime insisted. 'We don't seem to have any good ideas of our own.'

'All right. But remember, you insisted,' she told them primly. 'Now look, and you tell me if I say anything wrong, please.' They both nodded. 'To begin with, your coffee bushes are all planted in rows down the side of the mountain. Beautifully straight rows. Right so far?' They both nodded again. 'And the ripe fruit will fall off the bushes when the bush is shaken?' Again they nodded agreement.

'Then the next factor. You have plenty of water up at the top of the mountain?'

'More than we know what to do with,' Jaime commented. 'During the rainy season we just don't have a place to put it, and after the rainy season we still have too much. So?'

'So we combine gravity and water, and come up with a hydraulic system that will reduce your labour costs still further. Take a look.' She handed him her small sketch of the mountainside with her solution applied on it.

'What my cartoon hero would do,' she lectured, 'is to use lightweight plastic sheets to form a long V-shaped trough under the bushes, stretching from the top of the plantation to the bottom. Now, when your men shake the bushes, the ripe berries will fall into this trough. Right so far?' They both nodded. 'So up here, at the top,' she demonstrated, 'you install a little irrigation pipe to bring water—just a little of it—into each of the troughs. Now, the berries fall into the trough, the water pressure, twenty-four hours a day, rolls the berries down the hill, right into wherever you want them to go, and you send the left-over water into the lily pond. Presto! Harvest without hands. How's that for a labour-saving device?'

'Well, I'll be dipped in molasses and rolled into a ball!' Jason turned fully around to look at her. 'Jaime?'

'It's worth a try,' the farm manager chuckled. 'We could do it in sections. And we could set up a test unit right now, while things are slack, and see if gravity will do the work for us! And I thought all cartoons were just wild imaginings!'

'They are,' Evy admitted weakly. 'It probably won't work.'

'Probably not,' both men agreed simultaneously, trying to look as mournful as she sounded. 'But I think I'll go get the ball rolling—er—the bean rolling,' said Jaime as he downed his drink and started into the house.

'Clever, Mrs Hart,' said Jason. He set his glass down on the table and came over to her. 'Clever. Beautiful. Talented. What else? Where did you learn to sketch?'

'I don't know,' she said, ducking her head. 'I always could, to some degree. But when I went into High School we had an art teacher—a Dominican nun, actually—and she thought—well, she helped me. And then I went to night school for a time, and I guess that's it.'

'Do you do anything with oils or watercolours?'

'I—no, that's beyond me. I only do things that require a short time for accomplishment.'

'That's an interesting statement. How come?'

Evy shrugged her shoulders, unwilling to reveal anything more about herself. He knows I live from day to day, she told herself. Why would he expect me to take on a responsibility that might run for—months? Or years?

When Jason realized she was not going to answer he took the glass out of her hands, pulled her to her feet, and gently kissed her. There was no fire, as there had been in the morning, just a cool comforting contact. And when he let her go he was laughing.

'You *are* a morning person, aren't you!' Before she could hit him he wandered off to dress for dinner.

That night the dinner table was lively. Francisca was back from her little trip, and both Ramón and Jaime joined them for the meal, which was a considerable surprise—tender medium-rare steaks, smothered in mushrooms, with a small salad plate, and of course the inevitable serving of rice and beans.

'I went into San Juan today,' Francisca threw into the conversation. 'I have a few more touches to add to the gowns for the Governor's Ball!'

'But of course nothing could keep you from our company,' said Jaime, just a little sarcastically. She took up the gauge.

'Some of your company,' she qualified. 'And of course it was a problem, driving all the way. Now if Jason had loaned me his helicopter, it would have been much easier.'

'Too bad,' commented Jason. 'You didn't tell us where you were going today. If you'd waited, we would all be able to fly in to the city. Mrs Hart has to see a man in the Federal Building. We'll be going in early tomorrow.'

'Oh, I do?' Evy queried.

'What time are you leaving?' asked Francisca.

'Yes, you do,' he answered both at the same time. 'And I think we should leave here about nine o'clock. Your appointment is at eleven.'

'It doesn't take that long to go by chopper,' Francisca pointed out. She seemed to be unusually interested. Her eyes were sparking as they had not done before.

'Well, I thought we might see one or two of the sights in the old city,' he responded. 'Maybe we could go to the cathedral, and over to El Moro. Things like that.'

'Don't you think I should know the name of the person I have this so-called appointment with?' asked Evy.

He patted her left hand, effectively ending her attempt to feed herself one-handedly. 'No,' he said, and smiled at her.

'Why, you've got a lot—' she started to yell at him, then thought better of it and kept silent.

'I've got what?'

'You've got—to cut up the rest of my steak for me,'

she said in a much lower voice. 'I can't do it with one hand.'

He took her plate in front of him and used his own knife to slice the tender meat into bite-sized portions. 'There. Does that suit, child?' Evy glared at him. He seemed to be glare-proof. But not foot-proof. She was wearing a pair of high-heeled shoes, with pointed toes, and when she slammed one of the points into his ankle while he was sampling the red wine, he almost choked.

'Did it go down the wrong pipe?' She handed him her napkin and did her best to appear as innocent as possible.

'Yes, I think so,' he gasped. 'I must remember not to play children's games at the table. Coffee in the living room, Delfinia?'

'I think I must be excused,' said Francisca as they all rose and started out. And that was the last they saw of her for the rest of the evening.

At eight o'clock the next morning Evy was still debating. Just what does a girl wear for an appointment with 'I don't know who,' after a helicopter ride from here to 'I don't know where'? Maria gave her a verbal push.

'You don't wear a dress to fly all up in the air,' she pronounced. Which was some sort of change, for of all things Maria cherished the idea that women wear dresses, and men wear pants!

'You think I should wear slacks?' asked Evy. 'A helicopter is a very refined vehicle, I think.'

'I don't mean the helichopper flies all up in the air,' her *dueña* explained. 'I mean the dress flies all up in the air, when you go on that whirlybird thing. I see it on the television. Wear something nice—no blue jeans—and comb your hair careful. Is better in braids, no?'

And so it was white slacks, a prim white blouse with a lace collar, and the braids, no! All securely fastened in a coronet around the rim of Evy's head.

'And a sweater,' Maria insisted. 'It gets cold to come back to the mountains in the night time.'

'And how about an umbrella?' asked Evy. 'It looks pretty cloudy to the west.'

'Umbrella!' Maria shook with laughter. 'In the dry season?'

'But it rains. You know it rains in the dry season!'

'Yes—*seguro*. For ten, maybe fifteen minutes. Nobody uses umbrellas. When it starts to rain, everybody stop, goes inside someplace—store restaurant, anything. And pretty soon it stops!'

'Huh!' snapped Evy, trying to select an appropriate sweater. 'And suppose you're in a hurry, and it starts to rain?'

'Nobody in Puerto Rico is in that much hurry,' Maria replied. 'You need to learn, *linda. Poco a poco*, no?— little bit at a time. But not now. I hear the motor on the helichopper, no? And that Don Jason, he is not the man to wait. Especially not for no woman, huh! *Vamos!*'

Evy was still trying to sort all that out as she settled back in the front seat of the machine and waited on events. Jason was being solicitous. He strapped her in, checking each buckle with extra care. His busy hands brushed across her breasts twice in the doing, but it was obviously an accident. At least that was what she told herself. Jaime climbed in the back, along with a young *jibaro* who was introduced as Rafael. A very big, pleasant young man, Evy noted. And before she could make anything of that, Jason manipulated some levers on his side of the cabin, the whistling blades rose to a crescendo, and something snatched them up and away from the island.

They went straight up, until well clear of the mountainside, then circled out over the Caribbean to gather even more altitude. Evy held both hands on her stomach, not at all sure that she had brought that valuable portion with her.

Jason had crowned her with a headset and a microphone, nevertheless she was surprised when his voice filled her ear in a casual conversational way. 'We're at five thousand feet,' he told her. 'We have to approach the airport from the east, and that means flying around the peak at El Yunque. Take a look as we go by!'

She was glued to the window. For the first time she saw all the island. One hundred miles long, thirty-five miles wide, it was the last and smallest of the Greater Antilles, a chain of island including Cuba, Hispaniola, and Puerto Rico, making a shelter that divided the Atlantic Ocean from the Caribbean Sea. At their height she could see the central *cordillera*, the mountain chain that ran east and west, dividing the island into two separate lands. That to the north of the mountains was a gentle slope down to wide sea-coast flatlands, while to the south of the *cordillera* the mountains sloped more steeply to a narrow shelf of beaches, with occasional wide valleys.

Dead ahead of them, too, she could see the vast sprawl that was Greater San Juan. Once a tiny old walled city, isolated on a separate island, the city now spread across the *barrios* of Santurce and Rio Piedras, meshing them into an industrial and business complex that contained almost a third of the island's population. And as the helicopter approached the Naval Air Station, waiting for landing instructions, she could see the cumbersome line of modern hotels and casinos that had sprung up along the wide sweep of the white beaches, all powered by the tourist and gambling dollar.

Eventually they took their turn in the elephant walk of helicopters waiting to land at Isla Grande, and grounded within a circle to which ground crews directed them. Naturally, there was a car waiting for them, a big air-conditioned limousine, and a gaggle of Naval personnel, all stiff and correct in their white uniforms. 'Don Jason is a Captain in the Naval Reserve,' Jaime whispered in her ear. 'Otherwise we don't even get to land on the naval base, and it takes much waiting time to land over at the International Airport. Nice, huh?'

'Nice.' She smiled back at him as she settled back in the cool comfort of the car. Although it was springtime, the heat and the humidity in the city always seemed to be fifteen degrees worse than in the mountains. Jason drove. He wheeled the car out on to the Munoz Riviera Expressway, and they headed towards the city. Evy peered out of the back window as they sped away.

'There's a car following us,' she reported, and Jason peered into his rear-view mirror. Jaime squirmed around in the back seat and took a good look.

'There'd better be a car back there,' said Jason.

Evy looked thoughtfully at the back of his head. So assured, so arrogant. 'Jason, should I be frightened of something?'

'Are you?'

'No. I—somehow—I seem to feel quite safe when you're close by.'

'Well, that's another step forward,' he chuckled. He took one hand off the wheel and reached back. She put her hand in his, treasuring the momentary contact before he withdrew. 'There's nothing to be frightened of, as long as you're not alone,' he told her. 'And that ought to be a police car following us.'

'It isn't,' reported Jaime. 'The police don't use that kind of car. But it looks as if there is a police car in back of *them*.'

The driver of the car behind them seemed to have made the same deduction, for as Jason's car slowed to make the turn into Ponce de León Avenue, the car behind them dropped back, turned off one street earlier, and disappeared with screaming tyres.

'Damn!' Jason banged his hand down on the steering wheel in frustration. 'They knew! Bloody hell, they knew! We've got a leak inside our own house. They knew we were coming!'

'They've gone.' Jaime tried to pacify him. 'There's no harm done. They don't want to hurt her.'

'Of course they don't,' Jason said grimly. 'All they want to do is to ask her a few polite questions. Then after that they might consider hurting her!'

'What in the world are you talking about?' Evy's voice was two notes higher than usual. I'm not afraid, she told herself. I will not be turned into a rabbit again. Keep cool!

'You'll see when you get to your appointment,' said Jason, now fully in control of his temper. 'Some of this will be explained, Evy. Don't let it bother you now. And I think we had better got directly to your appointment.' He leaned over and whispered a few words into a microphone on the dashboard. In no time at all they crossed the Puente San Antonio, and were driving down the broad Avenida Ponce de León, by the Munoz Rivera park, the Capitol building, the green space of the Plaza Colón, until finally they turned off and dived into the narrow cobblestoned streets of the old city. They drew up on the Calle Recinto Sur, and parked on the kerb.

'This is the old Federal building,' Jason told her. She started to get out, but Jaime held her arm, watching the window. The police car behind them disgorged three husky men, who were quickly joined by Jason and Rafael. Between them they inspected the block, the doors to the building, and looked every passer-by up and down. At last Jason leaned into the car. 'All clear,' he said.

Jaime squeezed by Evy and got out on the sidewalk.

Jason leaned in and offered her his hand. It evidently wasn't meant to support her, but rather to hurry her along. He almost dragged her across the sidewalk and into the building. Their escort had gone before them, clearing the way to the elevator. In minutes she was sitting across a battered old desk, looking at a very battered old man, and for the life of her she could not tell where she was. There were no signs on the door, no nameplates on the desk, and nothing in the room to suggest what it was that this old man did.

'Mrs Hart,' he said, clearing his throat. His voice was a cross between a growl and a whisper. 'You may call me Mr Smith.'

'Which isn't your name,' she snapped.

'Perhaps not.' When he smiled, his whole face changed. 'It will do for us to get along with. I knew your husband.'

Evy was so startled that she dropped her handbag and the weak catch sprang, throwing her worldly goods out across the floor. Jason restrained her from dropping to her knees to pick up the mess. She turned back to Mr Smith.

'You—you were in Cleveland?' she asked.

'Perhaps.' His smile showed a tooth missing directly in front, and the sparkle of an old-fashioned gold filling. She tried to relax against the back of the folding chair, only to find Jason's arm there for comfort.

'Did you know, Mrs Hart, that three years ago in Cleveland there was a—shall we say—disagreement within the Syndicate?'

'No,' she whispered. 'I don't know anything about the Syndicate. Nothing!'

'We know that. Nevertheless, there was trouble. The Chicago family tried to expand into Cleveland. There were several gang murders—nine, I believe. It shook up the leadership so much that for a time some of the little people got too big for their britches. There's nothing the Syndicate hates worse—for somebody in the organisation to go out on his own.'

'I—why are you telling me all this?' stammered Evy.

'Because your husband, Mrs Hart, was one of those little people.'

'But—I—yes, I knew that. He didn't know that I knew, but I did. He had—peculiar friends. But I . . . he wasn't the kind of man to think for himself. You must know that!'

'We know that. Not normally, he wasn't. Do you mind if I smoke?' Evy waved permission and he extracted a battered case and lit up. 'No, your Frank wouldn't have gone off on his own, except under the most powerful inducements. Do you know why your husband disappeared after you'd been married three months?'

'Of course. I got a court order restraining him. And I bought a shotgun!'

'Did you really!' Mr Smith seemed to think it was the best joke of the week. He laughed until tears came to his eyes, and not until he had carefully dried them on a crumpled handkerchief did he return to the subject.

'Marvellous—I congratulate you,' he growled. 'And that's why he had a problem! You've added something to my day, Mrs Hart. But that wasn't what I had in mind at all. Because of the—disarrangement of things, your husband, who was only a neighbourhood runner at the time, was sent down to San Diego to pick up a shipment. But when he got back to Cleveland, somebody had tipped the police, and he was arrested. But before they picked him up he managed to unload his goods, whatever they were. So he ended up with ninety days in the county jail for some little thing, I don't remember what, and they turned him loose. He went straight home to you. Do you remember? It was the night he died.'

'Yes, I remember. He broke in and knocked me

around. I don't know what else happened. I came to just soon enough to look out of the window and see the accident.'

It was all coming back to her now. All the horror, all the hatred, the fire, the—only the strength of Jason's hand in hers kept her from going over the brink again, into that strange never-never-land of the mind.

Mr Smith tapped his fingers on the table, trying to decide something. In whose favour? she thought desperately. Don't let him tell me anything more! Don't! But the bulldozer could not be stopped.

'Your husband managed to cheat everybody with that accident,' he said. 'One of the gang factions wanted to know what he knew, and the other thought he knew too much already. So they both had a contract out on him that night. He would have been executed for what he knew, Mrs Hart.'

Somebody in the room was screaming in a wild womanly voice. Evy could not imagine who it was. She was on her feet, wrapped safely in Jason's arms, and the screaming continued. She burrowed against him, trying to hide her head in his shirt, trying to cover her ears with her hands to shut out whatever it was she didn't want to hear. And then she realised who was screaming. Gradually the screams became whimpers, and then low moans. Her tears soaked into his shirt, and her whole body shook and shivered.

'You rotten bastard!' Jason snarled at the man behind the desk. 'You knew she was strung up. You didn't have to tell her that!'

'Perhaps not,' Mr Smith responded. There was not an ounce of sympathy in his voice. 'We never really know, in this business. Are you prepared to help me, Mrs Hart?'

'Is that what you want?' she sniffed. 'You want me to help you? You picked a strange way to get it. Are you one of those who wanted Frank dead?'

He had the grace to blush at that. 'No, I wouldn't stoop that low. I know the people who did, but that won't help. Your husband wasn't terribly important, Mrs Hart, but the stuff he carried was. Unfortunately, we still don't know exactly what it was he was carrying, or where the stuff is now.'

'And what's that got to do with me?'

'Simple, Mrs Hart. The Syndicate has now—re-covered—from its little problem, and the members seem to think that you know something about where that shipment is.'

'Who, me? I—I was only his wife. What do they want from me?'

'Information. That's what I want, too. We have a little plan to try to narrow the range of who is after what. Will you help?'

She waved a helpless hand at him, maintaining her desperate hold on Jason with the other. 'I—if I can,' she said.

He dived into the middle drawer of the desk and pulled out a series of glossy photographs. He pushed them over the desk towards her. 'Look at these,' he said. 'Tell me if there's any particular one of them with whom your husband was friendly.'

She took the photographs and screwed up her courage. There were twelve of them. Not until she came to the tenth did she see a familiar face. She pulled the picture out and threw it on the desk.

'Him,' she said. 'I don't remember his name. He and Frank seemed to be very close for a time.'

'Very good! Very good indeed!' Mr Smith turned the picture over and examined it from every angle. 'Very good, Mrs Hart. That's Alfred Schmidt—the very man.'

'And does that narrow down your search?' asked Jason.

'Considerably, Mr—er—Brown, is it? Are you perhaps one of us?'

'Not on your damn life,' Jason snapped. 'Well?'

'Mr Schmidt had only two interests in life, Mr Brown. One was women, the other was horse.'

'Horse?'

'Heroin, my dear sir. It will help. Narcotics are a very complex problem. At least you've given us another string to pull at, Mrs Hart. And now, Mr—Brown, perhaps you'd better get the lady out of my—er—office.'

Evy had regained control of her nerves, surprising even herself. Once again she was using Jason's handkerchief, and crying all over his shirt. When she mentioned it he tilted her head up with one hand under her chin and laughed at her. 'I've told you before,' he said, 'I've got another shirt.' Then he kissed her. No comforting compassion about this one. His lips swept across hers lightly, looking for a response, and when it came they seemed to seize and suffocate her in a blanket of wanton experience that sent her trembling against him, clutching at the nape of his neck with her undamaged hand, pressing hard to bring her hips and breasts hard up against his steel frame. And by the time she recovered, Mr Smith had gone.

'Was that horrible man really here?' she asked faintly.

Jason smiled at her. 'Perhaps not,' he chuckled. 'And now he's even got me talking that way. Say, you really *are* a morning person, aren't you! I must write that down in my notebook.'

'Oh, you—you fool!' She laughed back and did her best to cripple him with another kick on the ankle, which he avoided.

'I must have changed considerably since I've come to know you,' she told him as they went back down in the elevator. 'Before, with a screaming exercise like that, I would have wanted to go and hide for months. But now—'

'Now what?' he prompted.

'Now I'm just hungry. Could we find a McDonald's and buy the girl a hamburger?'

'We have them all over the island,' he returned, 'but I'm darned if that's what *I* plan to eat. Do you want to come with me?'

'That's one of the problems of being a girl in a strange land,' she teased him. 'I didn't bring any money.'

'On purpose, I'll bet,' he challenged her. She tried hard to keep the laughter out of her eyes, but failed.

'Perhaps,' she agreed, and took his arm.

'There's just an ideal place a few blocks from here,' he said as he led her off, up the cobblestoned street. The two husky policemen walked in front of them, while Jaime and Rafael brought up the rear. Was ever a girl escorted so to lunch? Evy asked herself. Safe in the hands of the District Police. She wanted to say something like that to Jason, but before she could form the comment he was urging her into a restaurant whose old-fashioned flavour was plain to see.

'Welcome to La Mallorquina,' he told her as he found a table for two, with their escorts sitting nearby. 'This is the oldest restaurant in the city. Now, do you really want a hamburger?'

'No, you fool,' she whispered at him. 'I wouldn't dare order a hamburger in here. But get me something I can eat with one hand, please, Daddy?'

'All right, smarty-pants.' He grinned down at her and very carefully arranged her chair to suit. 'Just for that, you get chicken again. Chicken Asopao. The chicken is well cooked, in a mixed dish with peas, peppers, and—of course—rice. Okay?' She nodded her acceptance, and managed to clear the tasty plate with only one hand, all the time wishing she could have him for dessert.

CHAPTER EIGHT

'I'M sorry about that, Evy,' commented Jason as the helicopter sat on the pad at Isla Grande, waiting for take-off instructions from the control tower. 'I had hoped to show you the old city, but I think it's too dangerous. These people know that you're in the city. God only knows what might happen. They want you pretty badly.'

'Well, I think we could have taken time at least to see the Cathedral,' she snapped back at him. 'I think you and Jaime and Ramón have some sort of complex about gangsters. We could have walked up the street and seen Ponce de León's tomb!'

'I don't think so,' he returned. 'You saw the street fight up the street from the restaurant. Did you want to get mixed up in that?'

'That was only a political brawl,' Jaime commented. 'A couple of Independencias were being too free with their opinions in a Statehood bar. Puerto Ricans take their politics very seriously. Volatile, I think the term is.'

'There, see! Just a political spat. We could have gone around the block!'

'I don't think so.'

'I'm beginning not to care what you think! You all act as if this was a 1930s gangster film. You've got some terrible paranoia about it, haven't you!' Deep within her there was a voice counselling caution, warning her to control her wild tongue, but equally strong was her need to strike out at this enveloping net of precautions that they insisted on throwing over her head. 'And that horrible man! You brought me all the way to San Juan to meet that disgusting man! Who is he? What does he do?'

Jason said a few words into his microphone, then dropped both hands into his lap. 'There's a delay. We have to hold until they clear traffic at the International Airport. And I have no idea who the man is. All I can tell you is that the President has established an inter-agency task force to work in the southern United States and the Caribbean islands. He works for some branch of the government.'

'What branch?' snapped Evy, caught up in her own rising emotions. 'Is there a Department of Garbage Disposal? That's the sort of place he would work!'

Somebody was saying something to him over the radio. He stretched out one big hand and laid it over her mouth, effectively sealing in the rest of her protest. 'Helicopter H34, Roger,' he said into his microphone. 'Shut up, Evy. Just plain shut up until I get us out of here!'

She sat up straight in her seat, shoulders squared, determined never ever to speak to him again—not for any purpose! She forced herself to stare out ahead of them, while all the time stretching her peripheral vision so that she could just barely see his face as he concentrated on the controls. She could feel his anger vibrating through the machine as he moved the throttle and almost literally jerked them up in the air.

'You don't have to be so—' she yelled at him, until she remembered her vow of silence, and then she was struck dumb by what she saw ahead. The helicopter took a wide turn out over San Juan bay, and directly ahead of her was the monstrous stone wall of the Spanish Empire's more important fortress in the Caribbean, the castle called El Moro. She had read about it in the advertising folders, but to see it at helicopter height was to be struck with the impossibility of its construction. And while she watched, Jason pulled the helicopter up another two hundred feet and hovered, so she could see the entire panorama.

The great bay was behind her now, its mouth sealed off by the tiny island on which the city of San Juan stood. In the medium distance she could see the change of water colour where the barrier reef stretched along the north coast. Ships entering the port were forced to travel some distance between the reef and the heavily fortified island before they could reach anchorage, and as they sailed towards that sanctuary they had to sail under the guns of tiny fort San Geronimo, past the slumbering bulk of San Cristobal castle, and finally, as they were prepared to turn into the harbour, they sailed in the shadow of the huge mass of stone that was El Moro. Its parapets, parade grounds, guard towers, and gun stations wandered all the way around the peninsula, until they joined with the remnants of the old city walls on either side.

'How could anyone ever attack that?' she gasped, as the sheer size of it began to sink in. 'Especially with a sailing ship!'

Jason locked the helicopter into its hover mode, and smiled over her almost childish interest. 'They tried, though. Sir Francis Drake, the Dutch, the French—they all tried. A couple of British assaults succeeded. But that fortress has been guarding the island since 1539. Inside the walls you can still see a shell from one of Admiral Sampson's fleet, when the Americans attacked the Spanish here in 1898. The shell went halfway through the wall and stuck there!'

'Then how in the world did the Americans conquer the island?'

'Yankee know-how,' he grinned. 'All the guns in that fortress point out to sea. The American army landed on the other side of the island and marched across to the castle's back door, so to speak. Not to mention that the

Puerto Ricans gave considerable help at the time.' He made another adjustment, and the helicopter moved out to sea on their journey home. Evy squirmed around to hold the fortress in view for as long as possible. When Condado Point obstructed the view, she turned around again, feeling as if she had lost something—something important.

'I still don't understand,' she sighed. 'All that stone—all that construction!—and in 1539. How could they have built it so large, to last so long?'

'Easy,' he answered gruffly. 'They built it with slave labour. Those stones are mortared together in the blood of the dead. Thousands died to build that thing. Thousands.'

She shuddered, closed her eyes, and tried to relax against the seat. She felt the urgent need to measure herself, her life, her goals, but the very presence so close to her of this disturbing man made it almost impossible. He was so much in and of the world, and she was a drop-out! He commanded respect and directed thousands, while she only wanted her tiny hidden corner—or did she? That was one serious part of her problem. Were all these strange urgings, desires, just natural responses to her need to climb out of her cocoon? And if they were, was she prepared to do so? For years she had hidden from herself the knowledge of her husband's life in Cleveland. And now this constant persecution. Was it really some paranoia that affected Jason? Or did he have some knowledge beyond hers that made it real? Some knowledge, perhaps gained from the horrible little man they had met this morning? A snatch of conversation haunted her. 'Thousands were driven to their death to build that fortress.' As I am being driven now? she asked herself. Why does Jason really want me to stay at the *finca*? Why is Francisca there? Why?

It was all too much for a tired, frightened mind to

handle. She grasped at tiny tendrils of thoughts, but they all eluded her. Lulled by the constant roar of the jet-turbine engine, soothed by the steady 'whap—whap—' of the rotor blades, she dropped off to sleep, leaving her problems, as well as her life, in Jason's capable hands.

There was a slight change in sound as the helicopter swam up the valley of the Rio Blanco, and she struggled to wake up. As the machine tilted to come around for the landing, the sudden movement threw her against Jason's shoulder. He was too busy at the controls to react, and hardly seemed to hear her when, her face buried deep in the corner of his shoulder, she whispered, 'I love you.' There was no response, and as the helicopter grounded heavily on its skids she straightened up and moved away from him.

The landing pad was behind the house, hidden in the shadow of the second coffee warehouse. Rafael left them to go back to work, while Jason and Jaime, deep in conversation, preceded her up the path. Evy watched him as he walked ahead of her, squared shoulders, head up, his lean strong hands waving like any typical Puerto Rican, to emphasise a point in the conversation. As they came around the corner of the warehouse, Evy could see Francisca standing at the head of the stairs, a worried expression on her beautiful face.

Evy slowed down and dropped behind the men. 'I love you, I love you, I love you,' she murmured under her breath. And what good does it do? Francisca and Jason and Evy. He's in the middle, and I'm on the end, too late to join in the parade. What am I letting myself in for? More years of misery? Where can I run next? Samoa? Damn! Damn! Damn!

Because she was so deep in her own thoughts she hardly noticed when two of the big farm dogs, mastiffs, came bounding around the corner, affectionately aimed at Jason. Both he and Jaime were on the fourth step when the dogs caught up with them, jumping and cavorting like puppies, for all their hundred pounds apiece.

'Get down, you little monsters!' laughed Jason, as he stopped, bumping into Jaime on the stair. And at that moment the dogs jumped, pawing against Jason's chest with their massive paws. The sudden shift of balance was too much for him. He slipped, banged into Jaime, and both men, with the dogs intermixed in the pile somewhere, came tumbling down the steps.

Evy was momentarily frozen—just long enough to observe and be surprised. The two men were sprawled on the ground at opposite sides of the stairs, not particularly hurt by the incident. But Francisca, who had been poised at the top in her 'lady of the manor' slouch, screeched once, and came hurtling down the stairs to comfort—Jaime.

'Good lord,' Evy snapped as she hurried towards Jason, 'are you hurt?'

'Nothing injured but my dignity,' he laughed. 'Get at least one of these monsters off me, will you?'

Evy bent to the task, using both hands to tug at the collar of the nearest dog. The animal, not admitting to trespass, was wagging at both ends. The tail beat down on Jason's midriff with enthusiasm, while the coarse tongue scraped affectionately at his face. Evy tugged a few more times, while Jason laughed at the ineffectiveness of her help.

'Well, if it's that funny,' she snapped, 'you can take care of yourself!' She stood up and symbolically washed her hands of his affairs—and stole a quick look out of the corner of her eye at where Francisca, sitting on the ground in her expensive designer-model dress, was cradling Jaime's head in her lap and muttering in Spanish. Something that pleased him very much, whatever it was. With a big smile on his face he relaxed, closing his eyes, and said something in return. At which Francisca turned brick-red, jumped to her feet, and let his head bang down against the earth with a dull thud. Jaime was up in an instant, and an argument followed, all in Spanish.

As Evy stood there, astonished, a pair of arms came around her and urged her up the stairs, away from the argument. 'Come on, nosey,' the deep voice whispered in her ear, and they were inside the house before she could sort out her thoughts. But only just inside.

'Don't—' she struggled against his arms, and managed to break away. She was still suffering from the residue of the day's excitement—the mix of that horrible man, and her own admission of love. Her mind fumbled for something to say.

'What's going on?' she finally managed to gasp.

'You mean with Francisca? Hey, I told you—Francisca and I grew up together—Jaime too. We were all part of the same childhood gang, you know—like brothers and sisters. So they have this little argument!' He raised both hands to waist height, palms upward, in that indefinable gesture that Puerto Ricans use, coupled with a shoulder shrug, to indicate something beyond comprehension. He looked out through the screens at the pair below them. Jaime had locked a hand on Francisca's wrist and was towing her back down the path.

'Damn!' snapped Jason, but he was grinning. 'They're going down to the swimming pool to continue the argument.'

'I don't see anything wrong with that,' Evy commented. 'Nobody likes to fight in public!'

'I don't mind them fighting, but I had thought you and I might go swimming—to cool off before dinner. They can argue anywhere, but we can only go swimming in the pool—no, wait just a darn minute, that's not true!' He turned and stared down at her, raising a finger to brush a lock of hair off her face. 'How about it, Evy? Would you like to cool off? And have a little fun? I know just the place. Lord, I haven't been there for years. Are you game for a little adventure?'

As she looked up at him she suddenly realised that she was game for any kind of an adventure, as long as he was included in the party! She nodded assent.

'Then go get yourself into a bathing suit,' he said. 'No bikini. You need something that will cover your little— well, that will cover you!' He sent her off with a pat on her bottom, which startled her. No man that she had ever known had *ever* been that—familiar? But instead of feeling indignant, she felt highly pleased as she clattered down the hall, trying her best, once she knew he was watching her, to—Good God, Evy Hart! What are you thinking of?—doing her best to wiggle. Very slightly, of course. More of a sway than a wiggle—damn it, she told herself as she closed her door behind her and leaned against it for strength. The giggles rose and overwhelmed her. Evy Hart! 'Oh, shut up,' she growled at her recalcitrant conscience as she stalked across the room.

It took much longer than he had expected for her to change into her maillot—at least that was what the expression on his face indicated when she finally came out. But how can you explain to a man that it takes a great deal more time to dress in little than it does to dress in much? And what would his first romantic word be as he saw her?

'Sneakers,' he said. 'We have to walk up the side of the mountain, so you need sneakers.'

Evy stomped back into the room, discarded the white open-faced sandals she had selected, and forced her feet into a disreputable pair of sneakers—the ones she wore in the garden, for the most part. But her grumbles lasted only long enough for her to attempt to tie the laces, which is an almost impossible job when one has a hand in a cast. She came back out looking a little more contrite. This time Jason wore an appreciative grin.

He not only tied the sneakers for her, but slipped a plastic bag tight over the cast, and fastened it on with string and with tape. 'Has to be waterproof,' he told her.

They walked in the shade of the trees, going barely five hundred feet up the mountain, directly above the house. Evy could hear the sound before they arrived, the gurgling splash of running water. And when they broke out into the little clearing she could not restrain a laugh of pleasure. She clapped her hands in appreciation, and Jason grinned again—grinned like a little boy showing off his prize frog to his first sweetheart. They had come upon the river again, or rather that chortling stream that would soon become the river. It poised itself at the top of a fifty-foot precipice, and dropped off in waterfall splendour, to a deep pool at its base.

It was not exactly a waterfall. The stone wall, rather than being a straight drop, was a smooth slanted stone trough, pitching the water down at speed, at a sixty-degree angle. The spray of its landing caught the sun, and sprinkled prisms of colour on the surrounding trees.

'Come on,' he called, and grabbed her hand again. Lord, look at me, she mused. I can't move by myself. I always seem to need a tugboat to pull me. But she went willingly, smiling.

There was a smaller path up the side of the waterfall, almost hidden, the path disused, and so quickly overgrown by the insatiable tropical greenery. But it led almost to the top of the precipice, and ended on a rock outcropping that projected out into the falling water.

'Now what?' she asked nervously.

'Just watch,' Jason called back to her. The noise of the falling water blocked normal conversation. She moved back a little. He shrugged off the sweatshirt he had been wearing, poised himself at the edge of the ledge, gave a wild whoop, and jumped forward into the stone trough. Instantly the force of the water seized him and hurtled him down its length, then catapulted him out as if off the end of a children's slide, and dropped him with a mighty splash square in the centre of the pool. He came up quickly, brushed the hair out of his face, and gave another mighty whoop as he dog-paddled in place.

'That's all there is to it,' he yelled up at her. 'Come on!'

Evy moved to the edge of the rock and looked down. But her coward's heart was just not ready for it. She lifted both her hands above her head in a negative gesture, and crouched back against the stone behind her. Below, he watched for a moment, shading his eyes with one hand, then he smoothly churned his way to the side of the pool and vaulted out.

Look at him, she lectured herself. Broad shoulders, gleaming from the water dripping down him. Tiny waist, slim flanks, long powerful legs. Look at him. And her mind went back to the restaurant where they had lunched. Prime dessert—nothing better. I'm the only girl within miles—and I didn't bring a spoon! She hugged herself and shivered—from her thoughts, of course, not from cold. And suddenly he was there beside her, bending over solicitously, all warmth and comfort.

'You don't have to be afraid, Evy. It's a beautiful safe ride. Come down with me?'

How can I refuse? she asked herself. I'd go anywhere with him—anywhere in his arms! She moved close, hugging his wetness to her, feeling the pressure of his firm flesh against her softness. His arms came around her, pressing her closer, and just for a sweet second she felt the touch of his lips on her forehead.

'Now, both together, at the count of three,' he told her. They moved to the edge like one person. He counted. She pulled herself against him as if trying to move inside his skin. 'Three!' he shouted, and she could feel herself toppling over into the suddenly freezing water. But her death-hold on him survived the successive shocks, and when they both surfaced, gasping for breath, she realised that it *had* been fun. So they did it again, and again, until finally, exhausted, they plopped down on the soft undergrowth on the bank of the pool, and napped.

Francisca was the star of the show at dinner that night. Dressed in a low-cut black sheath, and wearing a choker of sparkling emeralds, she bristled with conversation, stamping on every attempt by Jason to introduce subjects in which Evy could join. The woman seemed to be lit by some inner fire, burning fiercely, and almost consuming her with its radiance.

Evy sat quietly in her chair, still not quite with it, doing her best to follow the conversation without much success. Jaime, she noted, was equally silent. He wore an expression that Evy had trouble classifying until she caught a look at herself in the mirror over the sideboard, and then everything clicked into place. Jaime was looking at Francisca with the same lost expression that Evy herself sported as she looked at Jason. Why, he's in love with her! Evy told herself—and was only very slightly comforted by the thought that now there were two of them suffering from unrequited love.

The dinner lasted interminably. Delfinia had outdone herself in the kitchen. 'You won't like it,' Maria whispered in Evy's ear as she brought out the soup. 'She's cooking all that foreign stuff.' And of course, she was. Roast beef, mashed potatoes, Yorkshire pudding—and only the *dulce*, the dessert, could be called Puerto Rican. It was coconut icecream over tree-ripened mangoes.

When they trooped into the living room for coffee Jaime excused himself, claiming a problem with the huge cracking machines that provided the final processing of the coffee beans. Jason seemed to be humouring his farm manager.

'I keep trying to tell him,' he said after Jaime had left, 'it isn't anything we do in the processing that makes the coffee what it is. It's all wrapped up in the altitude, the shade, the soil, and then the skill of whoever roasts the beans that make it all work.'

'You mean all that machinery, and all that work, doesn't change the flavour?' Evy was astonished by the admission. She had taken the time to tour the entire operation, and had been much impressed.

'Of course not,' he retorted. 'Look—when the cherry finally ripens, we've done all we can. What you have is a fruit with a tough outer skin, a pulpy jelly inside, a parchment cover, and two little coffee beans. Everything else we do has only one purpose—to get those two little beans out cleanly, without changing their content. But when the beans get to the hands of the roaster, then everything changes. The process makes both taste and chemical changes in the bean. And the better the roaster, the better the coffee.'

'Oh lord, I'm just sick of coffee,' Francisca interrupted. 'We have to talk, Jason. Do you suppose Evy would excuse us? We could go down to the garden.'

'Don't hesitate on my account,' said Evy, trying to sound calm about the whole affair. 'I need a second cup of coffee, and I have some thinking to do. So go right ahead.'

She said it all casually, but there was nothing casual about her thoughts as the pair of them got up and wandered down the steps into the garden. 'Don't they make a beautiful couple?' Maria had come out to pick up the coffee tray. 'Delfinia says they have know each other all their lives, no? Maybe there will be a wedding.'

'Good heavens, how would I know?' snapped Evy.

She was conscious of the elderly eyes examining her, but was too discouraged to continue with her uninterested act.

'*Ay linda*,' Maria said softly, and hurried away with the chinaware and utensils.

Ay linda is right, Evy told herself. Don't they make a marvellous couple? Childhood sweethearts. Dear God, does everybody have to make such a casual thing about turning the knife in my back? They're so obviously perfect for each other! Then what the devil is he doing playing around with me? Just sampling a little blonde to change his luck before he puts on the halter? That's what I thought in the very beginning, and now that's what it looks like for sure. A weekend romance. I love you dearly, Evelyn Hart. Hop into my bed. Until Monday morning, when I revert to real-time! Damn the man!

She was seething when the door banged open, and Francisca came in alone.

'Where's Jason?' Evy had not meant to ask. It just seemed to slip out.

'He's gone to see Jaime about something.' Francisca wore a big triumphant grin, and she waved her left hand back and forth as if drying her nail polish. 'Well, that's not quite true, Evy. You know how men are—when it comes time to do the dirty work, they always look for someone else to do it for them. Jason is a good man, but no better than all the rest. He sent me to tell you.'

Panic crowded everything else out of Evy's mind. She had not the courage to ask the obvious question. She just sat rigidly in her chair, her eyes glued to Francisca's swaying hand, where a new ring had appeared. A garish diamond ring, in a platinum setting, all worn proudly on the third finger of the left hand.

'I told you before,' Francisca continued with a musical lilt in her voice. 'The gold bracelet—you remember? Well, now Jason has admitted that he has been—enjoying himself with you, so we decided to do it up in the American way, as well as the Spanish. Isn't it a beautiful ring? And we've set the date, Evy. Isn't that wonderful? Two weeks from tomorrow. We'll be married in the Porta Coeli Chapel in San German. You must come, of course!'

'I—I don't think I—no, I don't think I could come,' stammered Evy. 'But I wish you both well. You've both been—good friends to me, and I—'

'You must come,' Francisca insisted. 'We *have* been good friends. You can be one of my bridesmaids!'

'Oh God, no!' Evy was unable to control her stomach. She struggled to her feet and made a mad dash for the bathroom, barely making it in time to lose all her dinner. As she hung over the basin, tired beyond compare by the physical reaction, she felt the warmth of a hand on her shoulder. Francisca had followed her, and was wiping the perspiration from her tortured forehead with a small towel.

'I *am* sorry,' the other girl said, 'but I thought it would be better to do it straightforwardly. Come on, let me help you.' She picked up a soft facecloth, soaked it in tepid water, and gently washed Evy's hot face with it. Then she helped the quaking, shivering girl over to her bed.

'Sit there for a moment,' she said. 'It will pass.'

'Yes, I know it will,' muttered Evy. Certainly it will pass. Just as soon as I'm dead, it will pass. Does somebody up there really hate me? She could taste the bitter bile on her lips as she clung to Francisca, eager for any solace she could find. Isn't that strange? her mind asked her. The woman who has won your man, comforting you? But then you knew all the time that he was *her* man, not yours. She told you early enough, didn't she?

'You're not angry with me, are you?' Francisca

sounded anxious. 'I mean—I never wanted to hurt you. You must know that?'

'Yes, I know.' Evy raised both hands in the ageless appeal for understanding. 'It's not your fault. You *have* been a good friend. And you did tell me before. But—'

The word hung in the air between them. But? The little word that signalled the end of all her vain naïve hopes. *But.* 'But now I can't stay here any longer,' she sighed. 'I must go.'

'I understand. Jason is leaving tomorrow on a trip to Santo Domingo. If you must go, that would be the time. But be sure first, Evy. I don't want you to go just on my account.'

'No—no, I must go. And not tomorrow; I must go now. Tonight. How in the world can I get down to the city?'

'Are you sure? Remember how Jason has kept you guarded up here. You must be sure.'

'Please. I'm sure, Francisca. Don't nag at me. I *must* go—and tonight. But how?'

'Well,' said the other girl slowly, 'I suppose I could drive you back to your own house—I have my car here. But if Jason hears about it he'll surely kill me!'

'I won't ever tell him,' Evy pleaded. 'Please? I'll call Maria, and we can be packed within the hour. Please!'

'Very well. But are you sure that Maria should go with you?'

'Oh yes, I couldn't possibly go without Maria. You will?'

'Yes, I will. Go and get yourself ready. 'I'll bring the car around to the patio and wait for you. But quietly. If Jason hears about this it will be my neck for sure.'

'I wouldn't want to do anything that would make trouble between you and Jason,' muttered Evy. 'You're both—you—I'd better get Maria.'

It took more than an hour. Maria, when she learned of

the plan, was so much against it that she shifted into high-speed Spanish to render her protests, and as Evy continued adamant, Maria insisted that she must consult Jason before they left. But luckily, Jason had gone off to a meeting in Caguas, and could not be reached.

So it was a very quiet group of women who finally assembled themselves in Francisca's BMW for the winding trip down the side of the mountain. It was ten o'clock when they left the *finca*, a dark ten o'clock, with high clouds scudding across the sky, and no moon. For a young vibrant person, Francisca drove as if caution were her only watchword, and it was ten-thirty before they came into the city limits of Santiago, and there was not a soul on the streets. Music and laughter drenched them in bursts as they passed some of the open *cantinas*, and once a *mariachi* band could be heard playing at an outdoor dance. But the little white car continued on its way, nosing through the darkness of the unlit highways like a ship searching for a safe port. Occasionally in the distance they could see the gleam of lights from one of the small farms close to the road, and the smell of wood smoke reminded them that the darkness was still civilisation. But only occasionally.

It was eleven-fifteen when they pulled up in front of the old *aduana* which had become their home. And it was only then that Evy was able to take a deep breath. Maria grumbled her way out of the car, rattling her door keys, while Francisca helped Evy set their suitcases and drawing materials at the front doorstep. Then, refusing the refreshments offered, the Puerto Rican woman was back in her car, and off. Evy stood outside on the patio and watched the tail-lights fade into the darkness. And what am I going to do now? she asked herself. There was no answer. She hugged herself, half crying, and stared out to where the cresting waves could be seen, even in the darkness.

Maria broke up her fit of despondency. 'Come in, *linda*, come in. The mosquitoes will eat you up, no?'

'It doesn't matter,' Evy responded dully. It would be easier if only there were a single star. Just some sign that that somebody cared! Almost as if her wish had been heard, directly ahead of her, across the Caribbean, a spot of light flickered, dimmed, then shone brightly at her. Maria came out of the house, bringing a shawl which she draped across Evy's shoulders.

'It is not good to regret,' Maria said softly. 'There is always a new path, tomorrow and tomorrow. *Verdad?*'

'I suppose you're right,' sighed Evy, 'but it seems so useless to—to struggle. I thought—'

'The Señor Jason, no? He has the—how you say—much feeling for you. You will see.'

'No, I'm afraid you're wrong this time, Doña Maria. He and Francisca—Señorita Molinaro—they're to be married. In two weeks, she said, in San German.'

'Is it true?' Maria appeared to be astonished by the statement. 'This is not what I hear in the kitchen. And where else in the house would the truth be known?'

Evy smiled at that one. No doubt about it, in whatever culture, the truth is liable to be known first in the kitchen, and only later in the drawing room! 'I want to walk for a bit, Maria,' she said, shaking off the restraining hand.

'You must be careful! Remember what Ramón have said! *Madre de Dios*, I have forget to telephone him! *Dispensame*. And you be careful, no? You don't walk away from the house, and you come quickly in!'

'All right, all right,' sighed Evy. It was easier to acquiesce than to argue. 'I'm only going to the edge of the water. No farther.'

She rearranged the shawl over her shoulders. Even in the tropical night, the constant offshore winds brought coolness to every part of the island except for the

crowded cities. She sauntered slowly down the little
unpaved street that led to the water's edge, keeping her
eye on the lonely star on the horizon. When she reached
the end of the road she stopped for a moment to take off
her shoes, then let her feet sink into the soft white sand
of the beach. She turned around for just a moment to
look at the little village behind her. The only lights
shining were in her own house. For the rest of the
village, there was darkness.

Once, she knew, the darkness would have frightened
her, as almost everything else did. But she had grown
stronger, more sure of herself, especially in the last two
or three weeks. She moved slowly down to the edge of
the water, when gently lapping waves fished for her toes.
The water was slightly cooler than the air.

'What the hell,' she muttered. She hitched up the
skirts of the long gown she was still wearing—the gown
she had put on so happily for the dinner that night—and
waded out into the water. The beach at the Playa shelved
very gradually, and she was out almost fifty feet before
the water came over her ankles. And there she stopped.

Frank Santuccio, she thought. I learned a lot from
Frank. He taught me that the world was a jungle. That I
have to look out for myself. He taught me that pain is a
great reminder.

Jason Brown. I learned a great deal from Jason.
He taught me that men could be kind, good, though
undependable. He showed me that there were *some*
paved streets in the jungle. And the only pain he had
to offer was all self-inflicted. He belongs to someone
else!

And that seemed to be about all there was to it.
You've learned another lesson, Evy Hart. What do they
call it? Another salutary lesson? So now, pick up your
marbles and go home—and start all over again. And
never look back, Evy, never look back!

So she did. She turned firmly around, waded ashore, stuffed her wet feet in her shoes, and walked back to the house. Maria was waiting anxiously for her at the front door.

'So, *linda*, you are better now?'

'Yes, I think so. For the moment anyway, Maria.'

'*Bueno*. I have made some coffee, and a sandwich of ham. Come in, my dear.' But Evy, like Lot's wife, was unable to follow her own dictates. She stopped for a moment to look back at her star, gleaming low on the horizon. It seemed to be sputtering! 'That star, Maria,' she asked. 'What's happening?'

'*Ay!*' Maria chuckled. 'Is no star. Is the beacon light at Punta Arenas, on the island of Vieques. Come in now, no?' The old lady put an arm around Evy's shoulders and almost pushed her into the safety of the house. Evy could hardly move of her own volition. A terrible weight had fallen on her shoulders. There was no star. There was no tomorrow. There was only yesterday, and who can live in yesterday?

She dragged her feet into the house, and followed Maria around as she fastened all the shutters, all the auxiliary doors, and shone a large flashlight around the garden walls before she locked the garden door. Evy watched, helped, but did not care. When they came back to the kitchen she sat at the table while Maria bustled around.

The coffee was hot, fresh. I wonder who roasted that, she asked herself, remembering Jason's lecture. And that, of course, would be the trouble in all the days to come. Everything little thing would remind her of Jason. She ate one half of a sandwich, to please Maria, then made her excuses and went off to bed. As she huddled under her sheet she could hear the sad crooning of a mourning dove outside the window. At least she thought it was at first, but common sense intervened. Mourning doves never sang in the dark of night. But mockingbirds did, imitating others as they did so.

'Damn this island!' she half shouted into her pillow. 'Nothing is every what it seems to be. There wasn't even a star! 'And with that she fell into a restless haunted sleep.

CHAPTER NINE

It took two days for the truth to really sink in. No matter what Evy wanted to do, Jason intervened. Not physically, of course, because since the moment she had left the *finca* she had heard not a word from him. But he was always in her mind. She forced herself to go back to her cartoon work. Sylvester the Seal and his companions were supposed to represent small-town America. But no matter how she tried to stick to the plot, it kept coming out with a Puerto Rican flavour. And when Sylvester picked up a new buddy, a fast-talking mongoose with a Spanish accent, Evy knew she was doomed. The mongoose looked just like Jason. His nose, his ears, his hair—it made the work impossible. And then the power failed.

'Is like this,' Maria said placidly. 'I hear in the village a car have hit the electric pole on the highway, no?'

'Will it take long to repair?' Evy could not help but be anxious, although there was no reason for it.

'Who can say?' Maria shrugged. 'They will fix it *mañana*.'

Evy stamped her foot, irate. 'Now see here,' she said, 'is that the *mañana* that means tomorrow, or the one that means maybe?'

'Maybe tomorrow,' chuckled Maria. 'Why hurry? They will fix it—some time or another, no?'

'So we need to find a lantern?'

'Or candles, *mariposa*. The only place to buy a lantern is in Santiago—and the *publico* is already left!'

'Candles! Of course. I packed them all away. Where did the movers put all those extra cartons? In the garage? Come help me look, Maria.'

'*Seguro*. But what are we looking for?'

'Candles! I packed away all my Advent candles. There must be five or six of them, and a big holder! Come on.'

It was not really the need of candles that drove her, but rather the need to be doing something. And hunting among the still unopened cardboard boxes in the garage was just the thing. She almost skipped as she made her way down the corridor, and through the high old doors that led into the garage. It was a large building, once used as a warehouse for the Customs House. Now, the dozen or so containers that held all her worldly goods huddled in one small corner, lost.

'Ha! The vandals, they come here too,' snorted Maria in disgust. 'Look how they have push and pull and knock over, huh?'

'That's not important now,' Evy returned. 'I marked on the outside of each one, but—oh, I remember now. Look for my collection of rag dolls, Maria. I put the Advent wreath under the dolls in the bottom of that carton.'

'Dolls?'

Evy pulled up short. Dolls? What was the Spanish word? '*Munecas*,' she said. 'Never mind, I've found them. Help me to open this one up.'

Together they tugged and pulled and twisted, until finally the stiff cardboard disgorged its collection of rag dolls. Evy fumbled through them, stopping occasionally to cuddle an old favourite before setting it aside, while Maria watched with discerning eye.

'You have make all these yourself?' she asked.

'Yes. I was never rich enough for real dolls. I made them so I could give myself a Christmas present. They were all wonderful companions to me when I was young. Oh, here's the Advent wreath. Help me tug it out, please.'

Working carefully together, they managed to disinter the ornate artificial wreath from underneath the dolls. It was a clumsy affair of plastic logs laid in octagonal form around four large candle-holders. The whole was decorated with artificial holly, and tiny red plastic berries.

'It does look horrible, doesn't it?' Evy said doubtfully. 'But it was all I could afford to buy—for our first Christmas, you know. I thought Frank would love it.'

'But he did not, *linda*?'

'No. Frank didn't believe in Christmas. But I didn't find that out until after the wedding. He believed in Scrooge, though. Now, the candles ought to be in a package around here—ah, here they are.' She pulled out another container, and checked to see that the candles and their spares were all safe.

'So there. Set them up in the dining room, Maria, while I repack the dolls, will you?'

In the end, however, the dolls did not get repacked. Just the handling of them brought back so many little memories that she had not the heart to put them away again, and came out into the living room about half an hour later, carrying all twenty of them in her arms, and laughing.

'Is good to hear you laugh,' commented Maria. 'Now you eat some lunch, no? What we will do with the dolls?'

'Why, I—we'll leave them out here on the chairs, so they can share the candles with us tonight! I *am* hungry. What do we have for lunch?'

Lunch was a period for placid relaxation. Then she snubbed Maria's invitation to siesta, mustered up her pitifully few hand tools, and went out into the garden. It was a peaceful place, just slightly overrun by tropical growth which had gone untended too long. The beautiful bougainvillea, planted to conceal the wire chicken run, had overwhelmed the run, the shed behind it, and half the open wall. Evy attacked with a will, using an awkward set of tree-shears. Then she started with the hoe on the adjacent vegetable garden, rioting now in cabbages, onions, and lettuce.

She did as much justice as she could, then looked over the carefully formed oblongs in the rest of the garden that made up the separate flower beds. They gleamed in their glory, showing the work of many faithful hands in the past. Hands which had nurtured this garden for meditation. Wives, they had mostly been. Wives of the Customs officers who had been sent here over the years. Wives, isolated in the tiniest of towns, who had turned inward to beauty. Evy had even found their names in the office, attached to years of careful germination notes. And now she planned to add her name to the list. Evy Hart, temporary custodian. She was down on her knees with the zinnias when Maria came out, trying to re-arrange the little flowers that had been set out as a border to the rose beds.

'*Linda*, you have a visitor. The Señorita Molinaro have come to call.'

Evy was more than willing to give up her weeding. Her knees were stiff from the unaccustomed work. 'I'm coming, just as soon as I wash my hands,' she called.

She detoured around to the back bathroom to scrub the accumulated rich dirt from her hands—and from the tip of her nose. But as she came out into the living room she was still bemoaning the dirt stuck under her finger-nails. Francisca, as usual, looked as if she had just stepped out of a bandbox marked 'Sporting Afternoon'.

'Mrs Hart,' she said as her hostess came into the room. 'I thought you might be having a dull time, and an incredible piece of good luck has come my way. I'd like you to join me.'

Evy sank down into one of the chairs and smiled as she tried to relax her muscles. 'Good luck? That's something in short supply around these parts. And I may share in it?'

'Of course. I remembered you were here alone, and probably bored. Jason is still in Santo Domingo on one of those tiresome business trips, and I ran into Pablo Dominguez. You don't know him?'

'I'm afraid not. What's he famous for?'

'Not famous, my dear, just useful. Pablo has a contract with the School of Tropical Medicine. Twice a week he makes a trip out to Monkey Island to feed the animals. Surely you have heard of Monkey Island?'

'I do remember someone saying something about that! The island out in the bay where the monkeys are allowed to run loose?'

'Just so. But it is a little island, you understand. There's not enough room for their food to grow naturally, so twice a week Pablo must go the island and bring more food—fruits of all kinds. Then he makes a mash out of wheat and corn, and they eat that too. Well, anyway, today is the day, and Pablo is willing to take us along. Wouldn't you like to come?'

'Why, I would love that! They're not dangerous, are they?'

'The monkeys? No, not at all, unless you go in the rutting season, and interfere with the families. Come along. There's no need to dress up. We have to make the trip in an open sail boat, loaded with feed.'

'I do have to change these jeans,' protested Evy. 'The knees are all black, and I have to do something with my hair. Give me a few minutes. He will wait, won't he?'

The other woman looked anxiously at her watch. 'I suppose he will, but do hurry.' Evy hurried, but it still took twenty minutes before she was ready.

Francisca continued to steal glimpses at her watch, even when they walked out to the end of the long rickety pier and climbed aboard the little centreboard sailboat

that awaited them. No sooner were they aboard than the
lines were cast off, the boat heeled into the prevailing
wind, and for the first time Evy got a good look at the
man at the tiller.

'You're Pablo Dominguez? A blond blue-eyed Puerto
Rican? I can't believe that!' The man seated on the stern
thwart was about five foot nine, thin to the point of being
skinny, with a skin so pale that it seemed impossible for
him to have lived on the island, in the sun.

'Me?' he responded. 'No, my name is Ray—Ray
Boone. Pablo was—detained. He asked me to make the
run to the island.' He spoke pleasantly, but Evy felt
uneasy, troubled. She stared at the man, and the boat.
They both seemed to be what they were supposed to be.
His explanation was acceptable. And yet—? She turned
her brooding face outboard and concentrated on the
thrill of sailing.

As they came close to the island she could see that it
was shaped like an exercise bar, with a hill on each end,
joined by a narrow flat isthmus. There was no pier. The
boat ran up on the sloping sandy beach that made up the
isthmus.

Without waiting for the other two, Evy vaulted lightly
over the bow and on to the strip of sand. The island was
covered with trees and bushes, but several paths were
clearly marked, and standing in the middle of one of
them was a three-foot-high male monkey with brown
fur, a long nose, and a completely naked posterior. He
looked more like a shrunken pugilist than a research
monkey. She was startled.

'Good heavens, Francisca,' she gasped. 'I thought
Rhesus monkeys were tiny little things that clung to
something. Look at the size of that one! He looks as if he
would like to eat me!'

'That's the bull—the patriarch of the family,' Francisca returned. 'Don't let him worry you. He's just come

down to see what goodies there are to eat—and he's entirely vegetarian. He meets all the boats, and after he gets his stomach filled the rest of the troop are allowed to feed. But first we have to go up to the house. This way.'

She gestured towards the path that led up to the top of the larger hill on the island. Evy followed, keeping a careful eye behind her on the adult monkey. Who knows when a vegetarian might turn cannibal? she warned herself. Ray Boone brought up the rear, empty handed.

'Shouldn't we be carrying up some of the fruit?' she asked him as she stubbed her toe on a half-buried root.

'No need,' he grunted. He was obviously not only out of his environment, but out of shape too, a man whose physique spelled city rather than country. Evy shrugged her shoulders at his curtness, and turned around to follow Francisca's dainty heels, until they broke out into a clearing at the top of the hill. A ramshackle house faced them. It was built of wood, but most of the roof had fallen in, and the glass in the windows was shattered.

'This will be far enough,' Ray Boone called out, and Evy stopped. Francisca had a strange, almost tortured look on her face. The door of the house opened, and a small brown-haired man came out. It wasn't the scowl on his face that frightened Evy, it was the switchblade knife he was carrying in his hand.

'Why, you—you're Alfred Schmidt!' she gasped.

'Too bad you remembered that and not where the stuff is,' the little man grumbled at her. 'Ray is from Cleveland too, in case you don't know it. Now why don't you just sit down here on the doorstep and we'll all have a nice chat.' He waved the blade of his knife under her nose. Evy drew back, startled, tripped on the first step, and fell.

'Yeah,' the other man behind her said. 'Sit down, Mrs Santuccio. Did you know that I was a friend of your husband?'

'He didn't have any friends,' she snapped bitterly. She was frightened, but angry too, and as her blood boiled, so did her temper. The little man grabbed at her upper arm and knocked her back against the building. Her head banged against the unfinished boards, leaving her dizzy.

'Cut that out.' Francisca suddenly interjected herself into the play. 'There was to be no rough stuff! You were just going to have a talk with her, that's what they said. Just talk to her!'

'That's all I'm doing,' Alfred responded. 'We're just having a comfortable little talk, aren't we, Mrs Santuccio? And you keep yourself out of the way, lady. Did you think this was a class excursion? If we just wanted to talk to her, we could have done it in the village. We brought her out here just in case some of her answers get—very loud.'

Francisca was as frightened of that waving knife as Evy was. She retreated a few feet, a worried frown on her face. And while Alfred had his eye on Francisca, Evy decided to act. Which was just another of those things an orphan learns. If you decide to fight, do it quick and dirty! With all her strength she brought up her free hand and ripped at Alfred's face with her nails, drawing a bloody line down his face from eye to throat. He managed an oath, and dropped his hold on her arm—at which point Evy brought up her right hand, still encased in the heavy cast, in a mighty round-house swing that banged the cast off the side of his jaw with enough impact to send him crashing to the ground. But his fall was only temporary. As Francisca moved forward to help, the little man rolled over, recovered his knife, and jumped to his feet. His knife-point was at Evy's throat before she could move a muscle. And at that point Francisca decided whose side she was on. She came screeching at the knife-wielder's back and battered at him, forcing him away from Evy.

'Get over here and help!' he roared at his companion. Ray Boone, much the larger of the two men, came up behind Francisca and grabbed both her arms, rendering her temporarily immobile and defenceless.

Evy, her head considerably shaken by her own beating, struggled to help, but was too late. The little man, angered to the point of madness, swung a wild fist at Francisca, sinking his fist twice deep in her solar plexus, and then, taking careful aim, smashed at her jaw. She collapsed like a pole-axed steer. Ray Boone released her arms and she crumpled to the ground.

'Damn women,' growled Alfred. 'Why would anyone want to work with a woman? Now we'll have to get rid of the two of them!'

'You wouldn't have gotten this one out here, without her helping,' Ray snarled at him. 'Stop making a damn mess of things. We've got enough to explain to the people back in Cleveland already. Now grab her, and get her talking. Hurry it up—that damn Texan might catch up to us any minute.'

The little man with the knife turned around and stalked Evy into a corner. She set her back against the wall of the house, waving her good hand in front of her. Alfred came at her squarely and slowly, but out of the corner of her eye she could see Ray trying to steal up on her blind side. He made only two mistakes. He didn't have the knife, and he arrived on target seconds before his accomplice. Without even thinking about it, Evy switched her attention to the closer man. Once again her hand flashed out, embedding her nails in the man's face, and slashing downwards to trail blood from his eye to his chin.

He yelled at the pain of it, and backed off from the unequal battle. For just a brief second, ignoring the command to run, Evy stood and watched—and as a result the little man caught up with her.

His right hand seized her by the throat in a strangling grip, while his left, wide open, slapped her until her head rocked. While she struggled to draw a breath, one of his feet kicked hers out from under her, and she crashed to the ground, winded, and now thoroughly frightened.

'All right,' he snarled at her, stooping over to bring her face closer to his. 'If you want to play rough, I'll arrange it. Do you?'

She sat mute, shaking her head from side to side, as close to panic as ever she had been, but held on the right side of thought by a compulsion—a drive that she had never felt before. Everything that Jason had warned her about had now come true, and, isolated on this island, the one strong lifeline that held her to sanity was pride. Pride in what she had become, not what she once had been. Pride in the thought that she must do something—anything—to make Jason, if he ever came to know, proud of her too.

'I—what is it that you want from me?' she gasped.

'Tell me where he hid it,' the man snapped at her. 'Where is it?'

She looked up at him, dazed. 'Where is what?' she asked weakly. Over his shoulder she could see Francisca stir, make a feeble effort to stand, and then begin to crawl away towards the path.

'Don't give me that,' he returned. 'Where is it?'

Her mind was working at a thousand miles an hour. Where is it? What is it? It went all the way back, inexorably, to Cleveland. What is it? Something of Frank's. Something that Frank had brought into the house, and then couldn't even find for himself!

'So what happens if I tell you?' she asked cautiously.

'Don't stall, lady. We have to get out of here in less than an hour. Just start thinking about what will happen if you *don't* tell me.' His palm opened and swept across her cheek again, rocking her head back against the ground.

'All right,' she sighed. 'It's in the house. But I can't tell you where it is. I'll have to show you.'

'Don't fall for that line,' interrupted Ray. His face was disfigured by blood, and he was in an ugly mood. 'Come on, Fred. I thought you were the one who could get answers out of a stone! Time's running out. Make her talk.'

'Shut up,' snarled Alfred. 'If you hadn't messed this up two weeks ago we could have been free and clear by now. I'll make her talk. You just keep out of the way!'

He grabbed Evy with both hands and pulled her up to her feet, pushing her back against the wall of the house and shaking her back and forth like one of her own rag dolls. Why, he's hardly bigger than I am, she thought as she tried to get her mind in gear. Over his shoulder she could see the last of Francisca, as the other woman slithered out of sight down the path. And then there was movement in the bushes on the other side, and her mind clicked into service again.

'Jason! Thank God you've come!" she shouted.

Alfred released his grip on her shoulders, whirled around in the direction of the waving bushes, and took four steps downhill! It was just enough movement for Evy to break away. She was ten feet down the path on the opposite side of the hill when the bushes parted, and two monkeys sauntered into the clearing.

'Get her!' yelled Alfred. Ray, who was nearer by several steps, whirled and started in hot pursuit. But fear lent wings to Evy's feet, and she careered down the path, almost bouncing from tree to tree, like an Olympic champion. Ray Boone was ten or fifteen feet behind her, obscured by the jerks and twists in the path. Alfred made no effort to follow her, evidently confident that his partner would catch up with her.

The run was exhausting. She barely managed a deep breath, wiped the perspiration from her eyes, and put her head down to watch for protruding growths that might trip her. She was almost back to the beach when she heard a noise in front of her, in the bushes. Oh Lord, she thought, another damn monkey! She had been shocked at their size when she landed, and just a little fearful, but now a greater devil drove. She aimed herself straight for the noise, smashing through bushes at full speed—and bounced off the solid chest of the man who had haunted her all these days past!

'Jason?' she gasped as she almost collapsed at his feet.

'And about time!' he said gruffly in that deep voice that made him part of her love. Once again hands lifted her up, but this time to swing her around him and pass her into the arms of the police detective, Ramón Velasquez. By that time she was able to order her feet to stop running. They had been treadmilling all this time, without actually moving her anywhere. She twisted herself around, and saw Jason disappear up the path and out of sight. She leaned back against Ramón for a moment to catch her breath, then broke free and started up the hill on Jason's trail. It took only ten or fifteen stumbling steps for her to overtake him. In fact, she came around a bend in the trail and ran into him again. He was standing in the middle of the trail, straddling the body of the man who called himself Ray Boone.

'Oh, Jason!' she sighed, and put out a hand to lean against his solid protective body. He looked at her and smiled, all the while rubbing his right fist into his left palm.

'Oh, Jason is right,' he said comfortingly. 'Oh, Jason almost didn't make it, did I, sweetheart? Our helicopter was delayed at Punta Borinquen, and Jaime and I had a tough time getting back down here. What did this—what did he want?'

Evy extended both hands in his direction, and he answered the appeal, sweeping her up in welcome assurance. She rubbed her face against his comforting shoulder, and her breath steadied. 'Why, I still really don't know!' She felt astonished at her own admission. 'I— he—'

His fingers traced the bruises on her cheek. 'He did that?'

'He got worse than I did,' she giggled. 'Jason, I hit him! Not this one, the other one. I hit him with my cast, and he fell down!'

'Hey,' he chuckled, 'whatever happened to Miss Fraidy-cat? You hit him? Good for you!'

'Good for me is right,' she laughed. 'I actually hit him! Oh, heavenly days. And he fell down!'

'Well, don't be too damn proud,' he returned gruffly. 'I hit him too, and he fell down.'

'Yes, I'm sure,' she said more calmly now. 'But I never hit anybody before, not in my whole life. And you've hit millions of people, haven't you?'

'Well, twenty or thirty, maybe. And I said I was proud of you. Now where the devil are you going?'

'He's not the only one,' she yelped at him, having almost forgotten Alfred Schmidt in the euphoria of his praise. And before he could stop her she was away, running up the path, teeth clenched, braids flying in the air. It was rage that drove her. Rage, and revenge. He was only a little man. Why should she let him get away with all that?

When she burst out into the clearing again such a short time had elapsed that the two monkeys who had started it all were still standing in the shadow of the bushes, trying to decide which way to run. But Alfred, leaning against the house waiting, had a quicker mind than the monkeys. He got up to speed in a hurry, racing away from the harpy who pursued him.

He was almost free and clear, until Evy whooped after him, and from four feet away launched a flying tackle right out of the instruction manual for the National Football League. She smashed into the fleeing man just as his knees, and sent both of them sprawling and rolling down the mountainside. They both came up fighting, but Evy had the bit between her teeth and managed to roll over on top of him, where she proceeded to mercilessly pound on his face with her cast. When Jason finally came along to pry them apart he found Evy sitting back on Alfred's stomach, a very satisfied look on her usually terror-torn face, threatening to permanently disfigure the man with the hard heel of her shoe!

'Hey, tiger,' he laughed, pulling her off her sacrificial victim, 'take it easy! The long arm of the law has arrived!' And so he had.

'My grandmother always said I had to keep in better shape,' Ramón complained as he panted up and applied a pair of handcuffs to the still-prone man. 'It isn't the running, you understand. It's the running uphill!'

'Jason?' Evy leaned back against him now, trembling from the after-shock. He put one arm around her shoulders, and used the other hand, and his handkerchief, to wipe her face. 'I did it, didn't I? And now we've got them all captured, and everything will be all right. Let me have that handkerchief, I'll wash it for you!'

'Stop babbling!' Nevertheless he tucked the handkerchief into the pocket of her jeans. 'I've never met a woman before who's so worried about my laundry,' he laughed. 'But I've got other handkerchiefs, as well as other shirts. And before you get back up on cloud nine, we haven't really solved anything, you know.' He grinned down at her, reading the desolate feeling that swept across her mobile face. 'But what we have done is to get our hands on one more piece of the puzzle. Come on, cheer up.'

'Cheer up?' she asked dolefully. 'You mean I might have to go through this whole affair again? I couldn't do it. I just don't have that much courage.' She stopped for a second to catch her breath. 'Francisca! I forgot about Francisca! What's happened to her? She tried to help me, Jason—she really did. She tried to help me, and they—just beat her to the ground!'

'Not to worry,' he said softly. 'Jaime has got her. She'll be all right. They'll both be all right. We didn't catch any big fish, but we'll—'

'It's not that bad,' Ramón assured them. 'We have a little man here, and perhaps we can convince him to lead us to bigger fish. Let's get back.' A uniformed policeman came down the trail at that moment pushing both men, handcuffed, in front of him, and the group started back to the boat landing.

On the way back to the Playa, in two boats now, Evy noticed the detective applying a little subtle pressure. He sent Boone, the larger man, in one boat with the uniformed policeman, but kept Alfred in the second boat, along with Evy, Jason, and himself. Somehow or another Jaime and Francisca had disappeared, and when she tried to ask Jason about it, he shushed her.

'What will you charge them with?' asked Jason as soon as the boat was under way.

'Something that will hold them for a while,' Ramón replied. 'Kidnapping, felonious assault—that sort of thing. Anything except Federal crimes. We wouldn't want them to go back to the mainland, to one of those nice clean jails up there. We particularly want to keep them in one of our Puerto Rican jails.'

'Might put them away for some time?'

'For a reasonable time. Twenty to thirty years, more than likely. Just think, Fred—' Ramón nudged the prisoner with his foot, 'just think. The next free air you get to breathe will be in the new millennium! You ought to be out in, oh—about-2005 A.D. How about that? You could be the hit of the senior citizens of the twenty-first century. Won't that be something?'

The man who looked up at him from the cockpit of the little sailing craft was not the dandy Evy had first met. His face was marred by their encounter, and he wore a bitter expression. All Evy's passionate fury had fled. She felt a sense of compassion for him, and said so.

'Don't be foolish, *señora*,' said Ramón. 'What do you think they planned for you, these two—and their friends? Once they found out what they wanted, then *vaya con Dios* for you, huh? They are like sharks. Don't get too close!'

'Damn you, you rotten bastard!' Alfred snarled at him.

'Oh, but I always speak well of you,' Ramón returned, laughing. 'And who knows, perhaps in a few months you could use a friend in court. A different friend from the ones you have, you understand? You know what your friends' next step will be?'

The prisoner followed his argument with rapt attention.

'The next thing they will do,' the detective continued, 'is to see that you don't live long enough to talk to us. So there's your choice. You can either talk to us now, and we'll protect you—or we'll tell all the papers you *did* talk to us, and we'll let you go. And you know what will happen to you then.'

For the rest of the trip Evy leaned back against Jason's strength, his strong arms wrapped around her protectively, as the two small boats tacked back to the long wooden pier at the Playa. Four more policemen were waiting for them there, and relieved them of the prisoners. Just before he was led away, Alfred called Ramón. 'I think you may be right,' he said. The detective broke into a wide grin, and walked off with the little man to the police cars.

'Can you walk to the house?' Jason asked Evy.

'If you keep your arm around me,' she murmured. 'Closer than that, though!' He made the necessary adjustment, and they walked up the street so close to each other that they might have been Siamese twins.

'For a girl who's been battered and bruised,' he told her, 'you look remarkably chipper. That grin is as broad as a Cheshire Cat's.' And a few steps later, 'You were remarkably brave—for a coward, that is.'

'Yes,' she admitted, very self-satisfied, 'remarkably! But I don't think I could do it twice in my lifetime. And certainly not without you. That's what made me so—sure of myself, you know. I wanted you to be proud of me! And now what do we do?'

'If I could ever get you alone somewhere I'd show you,' he threatened, 'but this obviously isn't the time. Look at this!'

'This' was Maria, moving down the street as fast as her tired old legs could carry her, and waving her apron in the air for attention.

'Oh, *linda*!' she gasped as she bumped into them. Evy grabbed at her on one side, and Jason on the other. 'Is too much for my heart, no? A man have come—a horrible man with a little poodle dog. I think to hit him with a broom, but he have a badge of office. Hurry, before he steal the silverware!'

'Oh dear, now what?' sighed Evy. The day was already twenty-four hours too long, and if it were not for Jason's ready shoulder she would have stopped Maria right in the middle of the street and had a good cry with her!

'Jason,' she pleaded over her shoulder, 'you won't leave me?'

'I don't think so,' he assured her. 'Not until you tell me

to go. Let's have at it. He can't be all *that* terrible.'

That's what you think, Evy told herself. If he as much as sneezes at me I'm going to hide under the bed!

Like three bedraggled musketeers they managed their way up the street, and in the front door. The dog was at them immediately—a tiny French poodle, carefully trimmed, wearing a blue ribbon in place of a collar, and snapping as mean a pair of teeth as ever Evy had seen. In a sudden burst of cowardice she dodged behind Jason's back and allowed herself the luxury of a screech that shook the ironwood rafters.

'It's only a dog,' Jason said solemnly, but there was laughter behind the words. He's laughing at me, Evy realised. Laughing at me! What that—I'll—

'Well, I don't know what to do,' Jason complained. 'If I pick up the dog, he'll bite me. If I leave you both on the floor you'll scare each other to death. Ergo, I pick *you* up, little darling.' And he proceeded to do just that.

Little darling? It sounded so nice, and Francisca was obviously so far away. Little darling! 'And how do you know *I* won't bite you?' she whispered into his very comfortable shoulder.

'I have exceptionally good hearing,' he retorted, and pressed her so close that she felt a return of that strange excitement she had felt the first time he had held her. She gave up all thought of resistance, and settled herself down in his warm arms, squirrelling herself as close as possible. Jason carried her down the hall and into the living room.

And there, with his dirty shoes up on her best table, smoking a cigar that smelled as if it had been manufactured from floor droppings, was Mr Smith—that horrible Mr Smith.

'This is the ever-loving end!' Evy snapped. She wriggled herself free from Jason and thumped her feet down on the floor. 'You are ruining my table,' she snapped at her unwelcome visitor, 'and squashing my dolls!' Her anger was running up the scale towards the bursting point. 'I didn't invite you into my home, and unless you have a search warrant, Mr—er—Smith, or whatever your name is, you can take your mangy little dog and get out of my house! Now!'

He grinned at her, and struggled to his feet, but he looked at and talked to Jason. 'This is the girl who's afraid of her shadow?' he asked. 'You'd better explain before she bites me!'

'Yes, I think so,' laughed Jason.

'Conspirators!' Evy exploded, beating against his chest with her tiny fists. He gathered them up in his own hands and held her still.

'Easy, Evy,' he laughed. 'Two more bangs with that cast and I'll need a new rib! I invited Mr Smith. And that's his wonder dog, who's going to settle this whole problem for us.'

'You did? He is?'

'Close your mouth, sweetheart, there are flies in the house.'

'Damn you, you arrogant—you—' She set both her feet flat on the floor, doubled up her fist until her own nails pained her, and fought herself to a standstill.

'All right now?' He sounded anxious.

'Yes,' she said softly. 'Tell me.'

'I think it would be better if we show you,' he said. 'Mr Smith is with a branch of the Federal Government, on loan in this area for a particular problem. His dog has a peculiar talent.'

'Let me show you, Mrs Hart,' said Smith. He moved over to the door and snapped his fingers, and the little poodle came immediately to his side and followed him down the hall to the kitchen. Evy, Jason, and Maria trooped along behind.

'We'll start in this room.' He indicated the kitchen. 'It's the last room on this side of the house. Then we can work our way forward. Here, boy.'

He took a small paper packet from his pocket and held it in front of the dog's nose. The little animal sniffed, then sat down, waiting for further instructions. 'Go,' Mr Smith ordered.

At once the poodle began a slow circle of the room, quartering back and forth until he had covered every inch at least once. When the search was finished, the dog returned to Smith's heel.

'Nothing here,' the man said, and walked out of the kitchen and into Evy's workroom, where the scene was replayed. They followed the little dog as it sniffed its way up the corridor, combing through each room as it went, and then into the dining room. Once again the little nose was busy, but this time, halfway through the search, the poodle began to scratch madly at the floor just by the middle of the dining room table, and whined. Smith moved quickly to the dog's side.

'Somewhere around here,' he said quietly. 'Either under, in, or on top of the table.' He bent over quickly, agile for such a clumsy-looking man, picked up the dog, and set him on top of the table. At once the animal followed its nose to the Advent wreath, now sitting in the middle of the table with its four red candles gleaming at them, waiting to give light. And there the dog began to yap excitely, fixed in one place.

'That's it,' Smith said quietly as he picked up his dog again, and dropped him gently on the floor.

'That's what?' asked Evy, puzzled still.

'That's what they've all been looking for,' Mr Smith returned. He pulled the wreath over to him, reached into his pocket, and pulled out a switch-blade knife.

'What are you doing?' His knife blade was cutting into the soft plastic end of one of the plastic logs. 'That's valuable! You just can't come into my house and—what in the world is that?'

'That' was a trickle of gleaming white powder that sifted out of the hollow insides of the plastic log. Smith, using one hand, pulled a handkerchief from his pocket and spread it on the table. As he dug at each log the pile of white powder grew larger and larger, until finally he had unsealed and emptied all six of the logs of the display.

'I don't—I don't understand,' Evy whispered into the silence.

'The end of your puzzle, Mrs Hart,' the man said gruffly. 'This is what they all were after. This is why your husband made a trip to the border three years ago. And either he, or some of his buddies, thought that with all the confusion in the Syndicate ranks, they could get away with "misplacing" the goods. But of course, now that peace has been declared among the Families, somebody remembered.'

'But—I—what is it?' Evy whispered again, her eyes glued to the pile of white powder.

'They knew it had to be in your house,' Mr Smith continued. 'They thought you knew all about it at the time. Heroin, Mrs Hart. Pure high-grade heroin. I would guess, with what we have here, it would have a street value of over seven hundred and fifty thousand dollars. More than enough for them to want it—and you—back. Not necessarily in that order, of course.'

'But—I *didn't* know!' She appealed to Jason, not to Smith. 'I *didn't* know! It was just an old left-over ornament. I packed it under my collection of rag dolls. But I didn't know what was in it. Jason?' Her eyes made an age-old appeal to his authority.

'I know you didn't,' he said, pulling her back into the shelter of his arms. 'And Mr Smith knows that too!'

'Are they going to be forever on my back over this?'

'Not a chance,' Mr Smith replied jovially. 'Tomorrow we will release to all the news services the story about how a public-spirited citizen—that's you, Mrs Hart— aided the government's agents in the recovery of the missing heroin. With pictures maybe. And that will be that. The Syndicate is a business organisation. It can't afford to run around knocking off innocent bystanders whenever something goes wrong. And now that the stuff is in our hands, you're perfectly clear. If there is any vengeance taken, you can be sure it won't be against you.' He made the handkerchief up into a bag by knotting its four corners together, and shoved it into his pocket. 'And now, if I wasn't such a horrible man, I would wonder where I could get me a cup of coffee.'

'I—' Evy's face turned telltale red. 'I—may we offer you the hospitality of our house, Mr Smith?' she said sweetly. 'Would you stay for dinner? What are we having, Maria?'

Maria was not yet convinced that the devil had turned into a proper dinner guest. 'Beans and rice,' she said, not too enthusiastically. 'Or rice and beans?'

'Nonsense!' Evy sounded very sure of herself. 'Stay for dinner, Mr Smith. You too, Jason. We'll have tenderloin steak, and asparagus tips, and—And what else, Maria?'

The elderly woman looked Mr Smith up and down, obviously still wondering why he should be offered the best in the house at the dinner table. 'You speak Spanish, *señor*?' she asked, and he gave his head a negative shake. Maria immediately broke out in an all-encompassing smile. 'In that case,' she continued, 'we also will have *arroz y habichuelas*, no?'

CHAPTER TEN

THE sun was warm on her back as she stretched out lazily on the towel. Jason was still in the water, a black dot on the blue surface of the Atlantic. She watched as he stood up and walked out of the water, a bronze Greek statue, muscle-carved, Apollo. In a moment he dropped down beside her, spraying drops of water over her nearly-dried maillot.

'Hey!' she protested, but her heart was not in it. It was already entrusted to his hands.

'Well, if you'd worn a bikini it would never have happened.' He snatched up one of the smaller towels and rubbed himself down. Evy could almost taste the wonder of him, and a shiver went up her spine.

'What kind of logic is that?' she asked. 'I don't own a bikini. And if I did I wouldn't wear it within fifty miles of you!'

'Say, what's happened to that puny little religious coward?' He dropped down on to the towel beside her and appropriated her right hand. 'This thing looks a lot better without the cast on it. How does it feel?'

'Sort of—naked.' She tried to tug it away from him, but he turned it over and scanned the palm.

'You have a very long lifeline,' he said in a very melodramatic voice. 'And I see by your love-line that you will meet a tall dark stranger, and have—six kids! The hand looks nice, naked. Too bad we can't see the rest of you the same way!'

'Now, Jason,' she snapped, 'behave yourself! That's why I don't wear a bikini. You—you drool, did you know that?'

'How about that?' he laughed. His other hand moved to capture her chin.

'Jason! Somebody might see us!' She struggled against his strength, but not enough to dislodge him. She knew she could do better if she really want to. So did he.

'Come off it! Look around you. It's eight o'clock on a Sunday morning.' Evy did look. The beautiful white sand of Luquillo Beach swept around the long curve of the beach, with not a footstep on it. The Atlantic breakers, slowed by the offshore reef, splashed gently at their feet. And behind them loomed the mountains, so close that they appeared to be within reaching distance—El Yunque, the long-dormant volcano; El Toro, the guardian of the west, and the two lesser peaks between them. In the distance, at sea, the tops of a guided missile destroyer showed on the horizon as the vessel made for the deep-water anchorage of Roosevelt Roads, to the south.

'What did I tell you? Two miles of unmarked beach, and we're the only people on it. Evy?'

'What?'

'Gotcha!' Both his hands snatched at her and pulled her on top of him, squealing. She meant to struggle—at least to give the impression of struggling, but he was tickling her ribs, and the proximity of him was too much. She could feel the muscles of his chest as they pressed against her breasts, the warmth of his thighs against hers, and his laughing face, so close. He laughed, until she slipped both her arms around his neck and cut off the sound with her lips. Instantly the atmosphere changed. A warning bell clamoured in her mind, shrieking for attention, but she cut it off and continued her mad pursuit of the strange sensations which he aroused just by being there. His hands rested lightly on her back, gently stroking her, feeding the fires, until she ran out of breath.

'What am I doing? she thought she was asking herself, but Jason smiled. She pushed herself up slightly, and tried to separate herself mentally from him, as she had done physically. Nothing seemed to work.

'Stop trying to analyse it. Let yourself go,' he said. But that was something Evy was not prepared to do. Nothing in her young life had ever been successfully accomplished by letting herself go. And she was in no mood for virginal experiments.

'I can't do that,' she said glumly. 'I really thought I'd become a practised hero in these past four weeks, but it's not true. I've had too many years of cowardly living behind me to make such a sudden change. I'm sorry, Jason, but there it is.'

'It's just too soon,' he murmured in her ear. 'I can see the devil in you, Evy Hart. All I have to do is figure how to get her out. Suppose we just talk for a while?'

'Okay, talk. When do we have to go back to Fajardo to pick up Maria?'

'Noontime. But you know darn well that was just an excuse. She had to come all the way home to Fajardo because her latest great-grandson is cutting a tooth!'

'I'm sure it's an old Spanish custom,' she said primly, not willing to ascribe any deviousness to the lady she both loved and respected.

'Huh! Sixteen grandchildren she's got, and seven great-grandchildren. How's about that for an excuse?'

'Numbers don't count when you're measuring affection,' she snapped at him. 'Tell me about Francisca.'

'Well, that's a switch!'

'Don't do that!' Evy slapped his fingers away. They had been probing at the strapless top of her swimsuit. 'Talk about changing the subject! Tell me about Francisca.'

'What keeps that up?' asked Jason innocently. 'The suit—what keeps it up?'

'Good moral character,' she snapped at him. 'It has the strength of ten because my heart is pure. Francisca?'

'What about Francisca?'

'She told me you two were to be married. She even named the church and the date—I forgot where. That's why I left the *finca*.'

'She told you a big fat lie, Evy. And you believed her?'

'Well, I—yes, I did. It sounded very plausible. From what I knew about you, I thought you were just the kind of man who wanted to eat his cake and have it too. But tell me really—why?'

'My, what a wonderful opinion you have of me! And I don't even like cake.'

'Not have, had. What an opinion I *had* of you.'

'You mean you've changed your mind since then?'

'Yes—I mean—I—oh, shut up! Tell me about Francisca. Why did she do it?'

'Money, I suppose. She comes from a very old family on the island—the best of everything. But when her parents died, there was no money, and things were pretty desperate for her. Francisca's talent is considerable, you know, but not topnotch. And then she likes the ponies. I offered to help her, a number of times, but she was too proud to take our money. So when the loan sharks put the pressure on her, she cracked. She never really had an interest in me, Evy. It was always Jaime for her, since she was twelve years old. But they forced her. She had to find some way to get you out in the open, away from all your protection. And the route she chose very nearly worked, didn't it?'

'But—she helped me, Jason. In the end, where it all counts, she did help me. What happens to her now?'

'Very simple. She and Jaime are getting married next week. And in the fall our company is sending them down to Venezuela to manage our coffee interests down there.

It'll all work out for the best, believe me. Any other questions?'

'I must have a million more. Let me see. How did you know I was on Monkey Island?'

'Ramón. He had a man watching you twenty-four hours a day. Unfortunately, Jaime and I got stuck at Punta Borinquen, and we didn't get the word until you had already left for the island.'

'But you certainly came soon enough!' laughed Evy.

'Don't you remember? I showed you one day. The Playa is straight down the mountain from El Semillo— by helicopter, that is. It took us five minutes to come down. I thought at first we would fly to Monkey Island, but Ramón wanted us to sneak up on them.'

'And that's all? Did they arrest anybody else besides Boone and Schmidt?'

'No. Things don't work out that easily, Evy. The team did manage to untangle a few leads that led back to Cleveland, and they did put the finger on a fairly large operator in San Juan, but that's it. The really good thing about it is that it got the Syndicate of your back. Did you enjoy the newspaper story?'

'I—it—well, you know I wasn't a hero at all. That reporter made it all up out of his head. But the picture was nice.'

'So are you.' His fingers were wandering again, but she had no intention of stopping him. It was true. The entire long curve of Luquillo Beach was empty, save for themselves, and besides, the movements of his fingers felt good!

'So now I've got a question for you,' he said. And I don't know how I'm going to answer it, Evy told herself. Not if those fingers keep on doing what they're doing! She moved away from him, sitting up in the sand with her knees tucked under her chin.

'So?'

'Evy, will you marry me?' And suddenly she felt as if she had crashed against a wall at full speed. Will you marry me? Waves of remembrance washed over her, bringing a chill that shook her tiny frame. That was just the way Frank had said it. 'Evy, will you marry me?' And she had destroyed him. Within weeks he was telling her how much he hated her. How much he—lord, don't let me think of that now, she prayed. But it was impossible to block out the memories—the names he had called her, the degradation he had forced on her, and all her fault. And in the end the frustrated beatings, the tearful rages, the—'Oh God!' she moaned. She struggled to her feet, avoiding Jason's helping hand, and she ran. She paid no attention to the direction. She just put her head down and ran, until she could run no more. And then she fell on her face in the sand and cried.

When the storm had passed, she rolled over, haplessly brushing the sand from her cheek. Jason was sitting beside her, staring, but not touching. She squirmed to a sitting position and stared back at him through tear-swollen eyes. She wanted him so badly, so much. But marriage? Then he really would know, and it all would come to an end so quickly. There has to be a way to have him—and not have him, she thought.

'Do you—want me so badly?' she asked softly.

'I can taste it,' he said morosely. 'I'd give anything.'

'It doesn't have to cost that much. If you want me, I—you don't have to marry me. I would—I will, if you want. You don't have to—'

'I'm not asking for a one-night stand,' he snapped. 'I'm looking for a commitment—a lifetime commitment. I want you, and children, and a lifetime of love, Evy!'

And so do I, her heart cried. So do I. I want you as much as you want me, but I dare not—I dare not take you. She brushed back the re-started tears, and returned his stare across the ten thousand miles that suddenly had popped up to separate them.

'I guess we'd better go for Maria,' he said at last. She nodded, accepted his helping hand, and left hers in his as they walked back to the car. He handed her in solicitously, as if she were a fragile ceramic, then walked around to the other side and slid under the wheel. He made a gesture towards the starter, then drew his hand back.

'Evy,' he said softly, 'just tell me this. Do you find me physically repulsive?'

'Repulsive? That's ridiculous! Of course I don't find you repulsive. If anything, you're too darn attractive. It's just that—well, marriage is—oh, please, Jason, take me home!'

He started the engine and spun the wheels in the loose sand. 'I wish to hell I knew what that bastard did to you,' he muttered as he drove back towards the city. Evy shrank away from his anger, crouching miserably against the door handle on her side of the car.

The trip back to the Playa was silent for the two of them, but Maria made up for it with a virtuoso demonstration of gossip about each of the members of her family. Jason responded from time to time, but Evy felt too terrified to speak at all. He stayed for dinner and then, after a long private talk with Maria, he went off. Evy went to bed early, feeling the need to cry herself to sleep. As she did.

When she awoke, feeling physically refreshed, she ate a hearty breakfast. Maria was watching her carefully, she noted out of the corner of her eye, but actually said nothing of importance. So, after breakfast, Evy went back out into the garden to puzzle it all out. There was a certain soothing symmetry out in that garden, that mirrored the years of love that had created it. There was careful organisation, and yet little incongruities which made it all—homey. For example, the rose beds, all carefully pruned, with their canes arranged in pristine rows. And then, set in the odd corner, as if thrown there casually, the old orange tree blossomed. The bed of Easter lilies was rampant in colour, but edged by sweet-smelling mint. The beds of carnations and geraniums, planted straight as a die, were shielded from the sun by a trellis overrun with flowering jasmine. And across from the rambling mass of bougainvillea that shielded the chicken run, a mass of clinging ivy vines concealed the cement tower that was the cistern. For no good reason, Evy's hands started weeding in the rose bed, her movements mechanical, while she argued with herself.

Will you marry me? Will you take another chance on the merry-go-round? If what Frank had told her about herself was true, marriage to Jason would be another disaster. True, Jason was not like Frank. He probably would not relieve all his frustrations by beating her. Probably? Of course he would not! But if he were disappointed, what would he do? She had no answer for that, so she put it aside.

The real question, she finally decided, was, do I love him? Yes, oh, yes, there could be no doubt about that! Then, if you love him, do you trust him? With my life! So far so good. Now, little Miss Mouse, would you *like* to marry him? Yes! Yes, indeed. Well then, what's all the argument about?

The argument is about—Evy stopped to rephrase the statement. The difficulty is, can I satisfy him? I know I can cook for him, talk with him, be his hostess, and love him mightily, but when push comes to shove, and we go upstairs together, can I satisfy him. Or will I turn him off?

There were tears of frustration in the corners of her eyes as she went over this one point time after time, because somewhere in the back of her mind a voice was roaring, 'Marry him! Damn the torpedoes!' And then? And then put on the best act you can. Is there a law that says every wife has to be completely fulfilled every time her husband comes to her? Fake it!

So, when Maria came out shortly before lunch, Evy was manufacturing smiles just for practice, and running through all the possible scenarios she could conceive of, so that she would have all her answers lined up in a row—just in case he asked her again.

Maria was grinning from ear to ear. 'He have come again, *linda*. He have say, she don't got no family, Doña Maria, so who could I ask but you? And I say to him, *es verdad*, like a granddaughter she is to me, no. And he says I want to marry up with her, and I say she is in the garden, and she is one very pretty lady, and maybe he got to stand in line if he don't hurry!'

'Oh, Maria, do you think—'

'I think you got dirt on you nose, but I send him out anyway. When a man talks marriage, you don't want to waste a minute, hey, or he change his mind. I send him.'

And send him she did. He came rambling out into the garden like a matador expecting to face a vicious bull, and determined to be successful. And when he saw her, with dirt on the knees of her tattered jeans, and her blouse all loose from the wasteband, dirt on her nose, pigtails flying in the wind, he immediately began his argument in a very loud stern voice.

'Now look here,' he said, 'I meant it when I asked you to marry me, and I don't intend to—'

'Yes,' she interrupted him, both hands folded behind her back, with fingers crossed.

'Don't interrupt me,' he said. 'I've been thinking about this all night long. Where was I?'

'You don't intend—' Evy offered.

'Yes. I don't intend to let anything like your past

experiences get in the way of you and me living a long and happy—what did you say?'

'I said, you don't intend—'

'Not that. What you said before that?'

'I said yes.' He looked startled, searching her face like a dog worrying a bone, looking for a loophole and unable to believe his ears.

'You said—yes?' asked Jason cautiously. 'Yes—what?'

She gave him an exaggerated sigh. 'As I remember it, you said you meant to marry me. And then I said yes.'

He was still suspicious. 'Yes, I meant it, or yes, you will?'

'Heaven help us if this is going to be a sample of our conversation,' she laughed. 'All our children will grow up to be lawyers!'

'Evy!' her name sounded like a war-whoop on his lips. It frightened the two parakeets in the corner, and echoed off the old walls with enough force to bring Maria running out of the kitchen. But before the echo died Jason swept Evy up off the ground and whirled her around in the air, all the while doing a war-dance with his feet.

'Hey, put me down!' she gasped. 'I break easily, you big overgrown arrogant lovable handsome man!'

'I don't believe I will,' he laughed. 'Not until after the wedding! I don't intend to let you move a step without me until we get it all sealed and legal-like.'

'That won't be too practical,' she teased him.

'What have happen?' shouted Maria as she charged to the rescue.

'Nothing yet,' he shouted at both of them. 'But it's about to!' And he proceeded to kiss Evy within an inch of her life.

From then on everything that happened seemed to be happening to somebody else. Evy drifted through the week as if she were an astral spirit, watching a mortal play being presented for her entertainment. Somehow or another the plans were made, the physical examinations required by Puerto Rican law were provided, and the Very Reverend Monsignor Hernandez, Dean of the Cathedral chapter, agreed to pontificate.

'It will be something simple,' Jason told her, so she bought a simple dress, a lightweight ivory, knee-length, with a fitted bodice and flaring skirt, all available from the stocks of Padin & Sons, in downtown San Juan. Maria insisted on a veil, and provided one from her family hope chest, along with a simple filigree gold coronet to hold it all in place. Jaime gave her away, Ramón served as best man, and his wife Eulalia was matron of honour. In the very last of the wooden pews, a very subdued Francisca came to watch.

They were married in the side-chapel of the Cathedral of San Juan, just a few steps removed from the ornate marble tomb that held the mortal remains of Ponce de León, the first Spanish governor of the island.

'It's a fake!' Evy nudged Jason and whispered at him as the solemn little procession started back up the aisle.

'What is?'

'Ponce de León. The tomb says 1909. You know darn well he died in Havana, Cuba, in 1521. It's a fake!'

'You're supposed to be looking at me with orange blossoms in your eyes, not at some dumb tomb.'

'I am, I am. But I couldn't help but notice. It's such a fancy tomb.'

'On my wedding day I get fancy tombs? Shut up and smile, woman!' And when they managed to get out to the sunlight, both were smiling.

The wedding reception was held at the Officers' Club of the Naval Air station, where Jason's rank in the Reserves guaranteed instant attention. Everybody came—all Maria's family, which made a goodly number, all the workers at the *finca* and the city office, most of Jason's friends and business associates, and about fifty other people who seemed to be strangers—but very friendly ones, for all that.

Jason parked the Continental just at the door of the Club, so naturally, when the pair of them came out to leave, it was raucously decorated with signs, soaped windows, ribbons, and tin cans tied to the back bumper. All of which might prove an embarrassment, and Evy thought surely he would blow the top of his head off. But instead he just laughed.

'Decoy,' he told her, and while the few partygoers who could tear themselves away from the bar cheered from the top step, he hurried her around to the side of the building and stuffed her into the little Reliant that was waiting there, unmarked. As they drove off under sunny skies, someone inside found a bugle or a trumpet, and was sounding 'Charge' as the newlyweds wheeled out on to the avenue.

It took some intricate manoeuvring to get them through the crowded noonday streets, but when they finally drove on to the Avenida Expresso Norte and were truly on their way Evy leaned back in the seat and relaxed.

'That dress is nice,' commented Jason as he watched her as much as the road. She had chosen for her going-away dress a little white sundress, with not much back, and hardly that much front, with a saucy swing to its skirt. Add to it a pair of low-heeled white shoes, a set of white bikini briefs underneath, and a very large white straw sunhat, and Evy Hart Brown was prepared to face the world!

'You look pretty edible yourself,' she returned. And he did. He had been impressive in his white suit, but now, in casual slacks and a sports-shirt, his hair ruffled by the wind, he took her heart away. 'Where are we going?'

'El Yunque,' he returned. 'I've got reservations in the La Mina Recreational Area. It's part of Luquillo Experimental Forest, the only tropical rain forest in the United States, as far as I know—unless you know of something else?'

'I don't know,' she chuckled. 'That's your department. I don't remember you being such a terrible driver before. Don't you ever watch the road?'

'Not when you sit there dressed like that,' he returned. 'I think I'll pull over to the side of the road and bite you.'

'You'd better not,' she laughed, trying to tug her short skirt down over her knees, but with little success. 'There's a sign there prohibiting roadside biting!'

'You made that up!' he accused her, but he did pay a little more attention to the road, and they arrived at their destination at two o'clock in the afternoon, right in the middle of siesta. Naturally nobody was available to guide them to their reserved cottage, but since Jason already had the keys, they shrugged their shoulders and moved on down the mountainside to their assigned position.

'Not much of a luxury stop,' he remarked as he helped her out of the vehicle. 'I'd forgotten how old some of these cabins are. In fact, there aren't many left. Would you have preferred one of the hotels on the beach?'

'It all looks lovely to me,' said Evy. 'All those climbing vines, and the lovely little stream coming down beside the cottage. Listen to it babble, will you. And look—Jason, look—that's a real orchid blooming up there!'

'Do you want me to pick it for you?'

'You'll break your silly neck,' she demurred. 'Let it grow. It looks so—so—oh, Jason!'

'What is it?'

'I—I don't know. Everything looks and smells so beautiful. What are you doing!'

'I'm carrying you over the threshold. Don't you know anything at all?

'Not much.' But she said it with a very satisfied expression on her face, until he closed the door behind them and she had a chance to look around. The cabin consisted of one fairly large room furnished as a combination bed-sitter, with an attached tiny bathroom and an area that might, in emergency, serve as a kitchen. It was the bed that held her attention, and suddenly the week-long daze passed away, and she came back to earth with a thump. She struggled out of Jason's arms, trying to stave off panic, and not being very successful about it.

'It's terrible—terribly warm,' she babbled. 'Didn't I see a swimming pool up by the restaurant? Wouldn't that be fun—to go swimming? Wouldn't it?'

He gave her one of those infectious grins. 'Don't panic, Evy,' he said. 'If you want to go swimming, we'll go swimming. Only remember, we're up on the top of the mountain!'

'I don't care,' she said. I don't care if it's on the surface of the moon, just as long as it gets me out of this cabin—out of range of this bed. 'Let me—where—I need my bathing suit!'

Twenty minutes later they walked up the path together, both wearing swimsuits and sandals. 'Stick to the trail,' Jason advised her. This is all volcanic lava around here.'

'Volcano?' Evy was fast losing all her courage.

'Don't be alarmed. It was a long time ago—so long ago that the lava is beginning to crack and disintegrate, leaving a great deal of thin surface. You could put your foot in a hole almost anywhere. And I don't want you to spend your honeymoon in a cast. Take my arm.'

She took it, clinging as if death threatened on the first

moment she let go. He smiled comfortingly down at her. There's no need for him to know, she told herself, that I'm holding on out of pleasure rather than fear!

When they came to the glittering natural pool she dropped the towel she had slung over her shoulder, and raced forward. 'Careful—' he tried to warn her, but it was too late for warnings. She dived in head first, and came up screaming. It was like diving into a tub full of ice! And there Jason stood at the poolside, laughing. Laughing! With a spurt fuelled by anger she struck out for the other side, pulling herself out with a strength she never knew she possessed.

'Why didn't you warn me?' she shouted angrily at him as she stamped up and down, doing her best not to turn blue.

'I did try,' he shouted back. 'It's a spring-fed pool, lady. The temperature of the water stays at a constant sixty degrees. Want to swim some more?'

She ran around the pool to him, intent on doing him serious damage, but before the fight started it had already degenerated into a laughing wrestling match, and ended when he had tickled her so much she was completely out of breath. When she pleaded for mercy he relented. But as soon as he stepped back a couple of paces she bumped him into the freezing pool, and, unable to keep her own balance, fell in after him. They played together for a few minutes, then raced one time up and down its length, and went, laughing, back to the cottage, arm in arm.

There was no 'carry me over the threshold' this time. They walked in side by side. Evy went straight to the bathroom, stripped and dried off, while Jason did the same in the bedroom. With her hair still soggy wet, she wrapped the bath towel around her and came out into the bedroom. Her heart was palpitating, her courage was screwed to the limit, but she meant to go down with all flags flying. She tried to think of something funny to say, but the words choked in her throat. He was waiting for her, arms spread wide in welcome, a towel loosely belted around his waist.

She flew across the room, driven by a want and need she had never felt before, and was quickly folded into his loving arms. As they met her towel slipped, and she found herself pressing her soft full breasts against the steel muscles of his chest. His lips met hers, and sealed her off from the outside world in a wild flight of passion which overwhelmed her panic. They stood glued together, as he hungrily searched her face, her neck, the upper swelling of her breasts, then he picked her up and carried her gently to the bed.

She was living in a rose world of fantasy as he came down on the bed beside her. Somehow she was breathing, but was not aware of it. He traced a trail of fire from her lips down her throat, and on to the hardened tips of her breasts, teasing her with his tongue while his hands roamed up and down from her waist to her thighs. It seemed almost as if he were drawing the soul out of her with the mad passion of his love, burning out all the dross in her with the heat of his fire. It was like nothing she had ever felt or dreamed before, and all her fears disappeared, sacrificed on this new altar of flame.

For mindless minutes she lay there, responding madly but passively to his inquisition, then her own hands began to wander, down the arc of his back, to the warm hard warmth of his hips, and lower, until both of them were moaning from the successive heights of torment.

When Jason shifted his weight on to her, and parted her thighs with his knee, she welcomed him with a fierceness that equalled his own, until they came together at last like two titans crashing at each other. She felt the sharpness of the pain, and he noticed it too, for it interrupted his rhythm, but it soon passed, and they

drove each other over the peaks of passion, then fell
away, satiated, gasping for breath.

'I don't believe it, Evy,' he murmured after some time
had passed. 'I don't believe it! You were married before,
and yet you're a virgin!'

She struggled to sit up, embarrassed beyond compare,
and yet relieved. 'I—I pleased you?'

'Good lord, girl, can't you tell!'

'I—he—he said it was my fault. That I turned men off.
He said—he—' She gulped, closed her eyes, and decided
to go all the way. 'He said he could do it with the girls in
town, but not with me, and it was all my fault—and—he
did try, but he couldn't, you know—and he blamed
me—and then he got so frustrated that he—every time
he tried, and—and then he would beat me. And I
believed it. I thought that—if we—you and I—married,
you would find out the same thing, but I love you so
much, I just had to try. You *do* see, don't you?'

'You were married to a fool—and a liar to boot, Evy.
But how were you to know? You pleased me very
much—very much. You are a whole lot of woman. And
just because your first husband was impotent there's no
need for you to carry around a load of guilt. Not any
more, girl.'

'Oh, Jason, you're so good for me. So good! But I—I
don't know anything about—about this sort of thing. So
you must tell me what you want me to do, please? But
did you stop to think, love, that maybe the first time was
just a fluke, and it might never work right again?'

'Why do I get the feeling that you're having me on,
Evy?' He tried to sound serious, but he was rather
pleased by the whole idea. So he told her a great deal,
then demonstrated that the first time was not a fluke at
all.

As the result of so many people being pleased by
others, they did not get up to the restaurant until ten

o'clock that night for dinner. There was one sleepy waiter on duty, who evidently had a feeling for honeymooners. The cook had long since gone home, but the waiter arranged for them to dine on left-overs in the kitchen, and joined them in the champagne toast, because he had the keys to the wine cellar. They ate well, then took a snack with them back down the mountain. A typical American snack—two bottles of imported champagne, and five bags of potato crisps.

They sat for a time on the little porch, and watched the third quarter moon disappear over the mountain tops. But by then the mosquitoes had found their range, so they withdrew under attack. And, there being nothing much else to do in the forest night, they went to bed again, and fell asleep—after a time.

It was the brook that woke Evy. It had seemed so sweet, in the late afternoon, running under their window, chattering, rattling, spitting at the world. But it was the sort of thing that should be turned off at sunset. And it hadn't been.

She lay quietly beside Jason for a few minutes, studying his face in the light of the earliest dawn, just stealing in through the screened windows. Asleep he looked—boyish—and her heart turned over. All mine, she thought. And suddenly, desperately, she wanted to ask him a question.

After all, she thought, why should he lie there so peacefully when I can't sleep, and it's all his fault anyway! Besides, the question was important, and she would probably have forgotten it if she waited for breakfast. She tugged at his shoulder.

He stirred briefly, and one of those big hands came up and swatted her away. 'Well, you won't get away with that,' she muttered. 'I'll—' She raised herself on one elbow and leaned over him, brushing the tip of her breast across his broad chest—to no avail. He grunted, and shifted to his other side. 'Damn!' she whispered. The question was becoming urgent—but for the life of her she couldn't remember what it was. She leaned over him again, and used the tendrils of her long hair to tickle his nose.

Bullseye! He opened one eye. 'Evy, are you doing that on purpose?' he asked grumpily. She hadn't counted on that—that he would wake up angry, that was! But she had come too far to turn back. 'I need to ask you a question,' she blurted fiercely.

Jason looked over her head at the travelling alarm clock by the bed. 'At five o'clock in the morning you want to ask me a question?' His voice registered halfway between a roar and a hurricane. She shifted away from him carefully, instantly revising her plan. 'So ask!' he commanded.

'I—you—are you mad at me?'

'Not yet, I'm not. Just give me a little time. What's the question, or was that it?'

'No—I—' her mind squirmed, trying to find something halfway between importance and disaster. 'I—we—what are we going to do with my house—and with Maria?' she stammered.

'For that you wake me up at five o'clock?' It was definitely hurricane time! Evy shivered and collapsed on the bed, trying to avoid looking at him.

'I—I just had to know,' she stuttered, 'and I didn't really think about the time.' She drew herself up, so she was sitting, with her back against the headboard.

'So all right,' he muttered, in that tone that men reserve for little children and congenital idiots. 'We're going to keep your house, and rent it out to Ramón and his family. Maria is going to live with them until the babies come—our babies. And then she's coming up to El Semillo to help take care of them. Does that satisfy you?'

'I—yes—of course,' she murmured as she tried to restore her injured dignity. She pulled him over to her and cradled his head against her breasts.

'Was that really the question you wanted to ask me?' There was still a glint in his eye, and she dared not ask now. Another substitute?

'You remember the night at El Semillo when you took me out to the garden and the *campagna de luna* were blooming—those beautiful, beautiful flowers?'

'I remember. They were beautiful. And so were you!'

'I—that was the night I fell in love with you, Jason. Will they still be blooming when we get back?'

He snuggled up against her, dropping a gentle kiss on the upper slope of her breast. 'Yes, they'll still be blooming. But you were a late starter, weren't you! You know when I fell in love with you, Evy Brown?'

'No, I don't. Are you going to tell me?'

'You can't avoid it, lady. It was in Santiago. I'd just run down this beautiful blonde with my car, and I got her into the seat, with her skirts up high enough to vote, and I leaned over her, waiting. And she opened those beautiful eyes, and said, 'How is the dog!' Write that down for your grandchildren, Evy. That's the first time in my playboy career I ever took second place to a rabid dog!'

'I think you made that up,' she whispered. His hand was on her kneecap, sending storm signals up and down her spine.

'Was that really the question you woke me up to ask?'

Well, she thought, I've tried everything else, perhaps a little honesty? 'No,' she admitted.

'Is this the question you wanted to ask?' His hand had left her knee, and began, very slowly, to move up the inside of her thigh, drawing little circles on her responsive skin.

'Yes,' she gasped. 'Lord, yes!'

'Hmmm,' he replied as he scooped her up in both his strong warm arms. 'Maria won't be out of a job for very long, will she!'